# DARK SECRETS

PLATINUM SECURITY
BOOK FOUR

KELLY MYERS

1

# HARLOW

I sit in a satin-trimmed chair at the edge of a cliff in Malibu and feel a smile tug on my lips as the celebrity wedding of the decade begins. Despite everyone in town wishing they had an invite to beloved starlet Easton Ross's nuptials to her former bodyguard and bad boy Jaxon Wilder, only a handful of close friends are present.

And, I am lucky enough to be one of them because I recently began working at Jax's company, Platinum Security. There's no question he had a rough time getting the business up off the ground and nearly had to close, but when Easton hired him to protect her from a stalker, his reputation and clients increased dramatically. Enough so, that he could hire more people, including me. And, now, we're like a little dysfunctional family.

The small office in East Hollywood is dominated by alpha males with plenty of deadly government training that provides them with a certain skill set to work as bodyguards, locators, investigators, troubleshooters and any other shady job clients pay them to do. They consist of former Navy SEALs, ex-CIA operatives and Jax himself was LAPD. Until he was let go for bad behavior. Although, in my book, revenge isn't necessarily bad.

Sometimes, it's deserved.

Until I came along, the ragtag group of anti-heroes was seriously lacking in one major area. Besides estrogen. And, that's someone with hacker skills. I had worked with Griff Lawson when he was CIA so he referred me to Jax and now here I am.

And, lucky for them. I don't mean to brag, but I'm the best of the best. I can find anything by digging deep online. The Dark Web is my best friend and coding keeps me sane.

Lately, the estrogen in the office has increased, though. These macho men have been falling like dominoes and meeting their matches. Love is definitely in the air and I glance over where Lexi Ryder sits next to me. Her fingers are entwined with Griff Lawson's and they are next in line to walk down the aisle.

On the other side of them sits Ryker Flynn, his gaze glued to Avery Archer-Flynn who is closer to the action, snapping pictures. She's a former CIA analyst turned photographer and Easton asked her to shoot the wedding. Ryker and Avery recently came back from a dangerous adventure down in Columbia and my head is still spinning from their complete 180-degree flip from hate to love to marriage.

But, there's no denying how good they look together. And, from what I know, all the men at P.S. had been haunted by troubled pasts and demons. Until these amazing women came into their lives and helped them pick up their broken pieces.

And, here I sit, by myself. No boyfriend. No date. Not even the possibility of a special someone.

That's kind of how it's been the past 30 years. I was never the girl who always had a boyfriend. I didn't go to my prom in high school or date fraternity guys in college and I never really fit into any of the cliques or social circles. I've always been more of a loner and prefer my laptop to a relationship.

Lately, though, I can't help but wonder what it might be like to meet that special someone. Problem is, I'm never interested in anyone for very long. A date here or there, maybe a hook-up, but then I lose interest and would rather be nose-deep online.

*Is something wrong with me?* I wonder. Have I been wasting my best years and one day I'm going to wake up, be 50 years old and completely alone?

God, that's depressing, but at this rate, it's exactly where I'm headed.

It's hard for me to open up, though. I hate being vulnerable. I've always been tough and a tomboy. I grew up with two older brothers, both former military, and they taught me how to be strong, independent and swear like a sailor. I'm not some weak, wilting flower who needs a man in her life or she has no purpose, no identity. Like my Mom before she died. I know who I am and I know what I want.

Unfortunately, I just can't seem to find it.

Honestly, until I saw it firsthand for myself at Platinum Security, I questioned if real, all-consuming love actually existed or if it was just something Hollywood and romance novels sold to desperate hearts. As nice as those movies and books may be, they don't keep you warm on a cold December night. And, even here in Southern California, the temperature drops in winter and I need to pull out my flannel sheets because there is no male body in my bed to keep me warm.

Other than my brothers who I don't see very often because they don't live near me, I've never had a good male role model to look up to. My Dad, the infamous Robert Vaughn, is a thief, a liar and an inmate serving 10-15 at the California State Prison in Lancaster.

Yep, good 'ol Daddy had quite the career as a successful thief until the law finally caught up with him. He's served five years of his sentence and I've never visited him. He emails me every blue moon, but I don't write him back. I have nothing to say to the man who broke my Mom's heart and left his family.

The ceremony is short and sweet. Before I know it, the priest pronounces Jax and Easton husband and wife. And, Jax drops his dark head and kisses Easton like she's the very oxygen he needs to breathe. When a lock of his hair falls forward, she pushes it back with a slim hand and they share a smile.

We all burst into applause and whistles as they turn and face us, holding hands.

"May I present to you-- Mr. and Mrs. Jaxon Wilder!" the priest announces.

I can't help but smile. I'm happy for them and wish them a lifetime of love. I know they both have had rough roads to love and deserve every good thing life has to offer. As they walk down the small aisle and pass us, Griff tosses Jax a salute. "Way to go, Jaxston!"

Only Griff, I think, and laugh. Jaxston is the name given to them by the media and Jax hates the attention and spotlight that they're thrust into at times. But, when you marry America's Sweetheart, it comes with the territory. That's why Easton made sure the wedding was small and quiet. If helicopters and paparazzi showed up, she claimed Jax would leave her at the altar.

But, we all know that is not true. From the look in his dark eyes, the man is head over heels in love with the raven-haired beauty.

I feel kind of bad, though, because I know Jax really wanted his younger brother to be here, but there's no sign of him. Not that I know what he looks like since he never comes around. Hell, Easton hasn't even met her new brother-in-law yet.

I don't know much about Sebastian Wilder other than he sounds like a wild card and a loner. A lost soul. Probably a lot like Jax before he met Easton.

Men like that...

I shake my head. I know them too well. My Dad was always involved with the wrong people and it didn't take him long to turn to a life of crime. He's extremely intelligent and likes to challenge himself. It's a shame he didn't put his talents to better use like my brothers and the men at P.S.

But, no, my Dad became a renowned thief. The feather in his cap and, ironically his downfall, was the job where he managed to steal $20 million in diamonds from a Saudi Arabian prince who's worth an estimated $14.3 billion.

Sure, that was a drop in the bucket for the prince, but to the average person, twenty million in diamonds is life-changing. But, I don't think my Dad did it for the money. Like I said, he always appreciated a good challenge.

The funny part is, they may have gotten my Dad, but they never found the diamonds.

And, as much as my Dad and I have always had a tempestuous relationship, I can't help but admire him just a little. But, I would never admit it. He's clever beyond comparison and charming beyond measure. I think I inherited his cleverness, and I've taken that cunning, quick-wit and savviness and turned it into the most amazing hacking skills you can imagine.

Dane and Rafe, my brothers, inherited his charm. No doubt about it. They're both extremely tall, athletic and possess a magnetism that can dazzle even the most cold-hearted women. Trust me. I've seen it.

I am the complete opposite. Zero charm, a little rough around the edges and I'm pretty damn sure that no man is stopping in his tracks to admire my boring brown hair and plain Jane looks. I mean, don't get me wrong. I do well with what I have, but when I look at Easton, Lexi and Avery, they all have some striking feature or two that sets them apart from everyone else.

Easton's green eyes sparkle like emeralds; Lexi's copper hair resembles the stunning autumn foliage; and Avery looks like a Victoria's Secret model with her angelic looks, bedhead blonde hair and cornflower blue eyes.

And, here I am. Harlow Vaughn, normally hunched over a computer, brown hair in a ponytail, dull blue-gray eyes probably behind a pair of glasses and not a stitch of makeup. I'd blame it on the fact that I grew up with two brothers, but Lexi also has a brother and she isn't nearly the tomboy that I am.

I just don't care about makeup, perfume and dressing up. I'm comfortable in my sweatpants, t-shirt and slippers. A little too comfortable and that's why I decided to finally pry myself out of my dark apartment and force myself to go into an office to work.

I'm 30 now, but the last five years or so, I'm kind of embarrassed to say, have been me and my beloved computers in the spare bedroom in my apartment. Totally absorbed in work. I have a lot of connections and people know to contact ShadowWalker, my handle, when they need a job done.

I don't want to be like my Dad, but, damn, how can I ignore the similarities? I spend all day on the Dark Web, involved in shady undertakings for clients who I never physically meet. We just exchange information online and I start digging through all my illegal back channels. After I find out what they need, and I always do, they wire me payment.

It's been a profitable, but lonely existence.

When Griff referred me to Jax, I wasn't sure at first. Working in an office and for someone else made me think I'd lose some of the freedom I have. But, it also forces me out of my apartment and comfort zone.

Jax assured me that I could work as a freelance contractor for them and that I didn't have to come into the office every day from 9-5 like a worker bee. So, I accepted his offer almost two months ago and so far it's been pretty perfect.

It's forcing me to meet people, getting me out of my dingy apartment and I'm really starting to make genuine relationships with the guys and their significant others. It's also making me feel a little more legit because I have an office now, as silly as that sounds.

The work is still shady as shit which I don't mind, but something about going into Platinum Security and sitting down at my desk with my mug of coffee makes me feel...more credible. And, appreciated. Jax, Griff and Ryker always make sure to let me know I'm doing a good job and that they wouldn't be able to function without my hacker skills.

And, it's nice to feel needed and appreciated.

After Jax and Easton finish their walk down the aisle, we all stand up and get ready to head over to Easton's mansion up in the Hollywood Hills where there's going to be a reception. I look forward to the endless flow of her favorite and very expensive French champagne Taittinger's Blanc de Blancs. *It's going to be quite the celebration,* I think. Especially since Ryker and Avery eloped recently and we haven't had the chance to celebrate yet.

Yes, I'm looking forward to drinking some bubbly and mingling with my friends for the next couple of hours. Then, probably heading back to the office for a little late night work.

I have no idea that my life is about to change dramatically and the dark whirlwind known as Sebastian Wilder is about to tear into my life like a tornado.

## 2

## BASTIAN

I lean my shoulder against a tree, staying out of sight, and watch my older brother kiss his wife. They make a striking couple, but never in a million years would I have thought my big brother would get married. And, to a celebrity. I haven't been around in the past year, but what the hell have I missed?

Apparently, quite a lot.

I've never seen Jax look so happy. His normally sad and haunted look is gone and he's fucking beaming. No doubt about it. My big bro is in love. Deep, head over heels, can't-live-without-Easton Ross in love.

I'm happy for him, but I can't relate.

I've never been in love. Not even close.

And, that's fine. No, thank you. Love is some intangible feeling that makes people do weird, out-of-character things. Plus, it makes you vulnerable and I hate feeling exposed, powerless and at someone else's mercy.

*Fuck that.*

I'm a screw-up, I know it and can admit it. But, falling in love would just make me a fool, too. Just as the thought crosses my mind, my gaze falls on one of the guests. I didn't notice her before because I could only see the back of her dark head. But, as Jax and Easton walk down the aisle and someone calls out, "Jaxston!"...she turns her head and laughs.

And, it's low and breathy and captures my attention.

Whoever she is, something about her makes my pulse speed up a bit. Her long, thick chestnut hair hangs down her back and when I get a look at her face, I squint a little, trying to see her better. But, she's too far away.

But, what little I do see, I like. *A lot.*

Whatever, it doesn't matter. I watch my brother and his new wife head toward a black SUV with tinted windows and mentally congratulate them. I know Jax wanted me here so that's why I made sure to come. But, the last thing I wanted to do was mess up his day and I have a tendency to fuck things up. Royally. It's the one consistent thing about me. So, it's better that I stay in the shadows where I'm most comfortable.

Out of sight, out of mind.

I want Jax to focus on his bride and their upcoming honeymoon. Not on his little brother who hasn't shown his cowardly face since Maddy died a year ago. I press my hand over my heart where her name is tattooed. *Madison.* An ache fills me when I think about her.

Guilt, too, because I should've stopped the assholes who murdered her. I knew them, associated with them, and I blame myself for her death even though it wasn't directly my fault. More like guilt by association. But, that doesn't make it any more bearable.

Maddy was the middle child, stuck between me and Jax. *Poor thing.* We tortured her mercilessly growing up, but she dished it right back. She learned to be tough, play in the dirt and didn't take our shit.

We were a close-knit group until our parents died in a head-on car collision when I was ten. Jax, Maddy and I went to live with our Aunt Rita and she did her best to try to instill some manners and religion, but we were a wild bunch. Jax and I slept during Sunday school and ran with the crowd who were known as troublemakers.

As the oldest, Jax believed his job was to take care of us and he took it very seriously. Even though we've always both been a couple of bad boys, Jax became a cop and was with LAPD for ten years. He always had this innate need to protect others so it wasn't a surprise. Then, when Maddy died, he fell apart. We both did, but he felt it on a different level. When the shit went down, Jax vowed revenge, went after her killers and almost died.

I ran.

But, that's what I do.

I don't like to stay in the same place too long or develop any serious attachments. I'm a loner who wanders. Maybe I'm searching for something to fill the void in me. I don't know. To be honest, I haven't found much to live for and that feeling of uselessness has grown more and more heavy over the past year.

Unlike Jax, I never felt any purpose or motivation to do anything. I wasn't drawn to a career as a cop or felt any sense of overwhelming patriotism to join the military or the desire to go to school and make a successful career for myself. Don't get me wrong. I like to make money. I just like to do it the fast and easy way. No muss, no fuss. Same way I like sex.

As soon as my mind turns to sex, I invariably look for the gorgeous brunette again. She's talking and walking with a petite, red-haired woman and some pretty boy who, after I squint again, recognize as Griff Lawson. We only met once, but I know he was the one who helped Jax track down Maddy's killers.

It looks like the mystery brunette is the only one who isn't paired off which I find a little crazy. *Maybe her boyfriend couldn't make it,* I think.

Suddenly, she pauses and glances over in my direction. *Shit.* I duck behind the tree and hope she didn't see me. I wait for a while then hear cars start up and figure it's safe to leave. As the guests drive away, I head back the way I came.

My motorcycle waits off the main road and behind a large tree. I reach for my helmet and take a moment to gaze out over the Pacific Ocean. The view is stunning. Almost as nice as that brunette who is making my blood start to boil.

*She's gone, idiot.* And that's probably a really good thing.

I glance down at my watch amidst a sea of tattoos. It was my Dad's watch and, if it weren't, I probably wouldn't wear a watch at all. But, it reminds me of him and, God knows, I miss him. I wish I had known him better. From what I do remember, though, he was the best. So, was my Mom.

I shove the melancholy away, slide a long leg over my bike, sit and zip up my leather jacket. As I pull my driving gloves on, I know I have to fight tonight. I'm not looking forward to it, but I need to make some money fast. And, after laying my eyes on that hot little brunette, I need to work off some steam and sexual frustration, too.

It's been awhile since I've been with a woman and punching some idiot into the ground will help relieve the stress.

I just have to win so I can get my hands on the cash. Because, I owe some pretty dangerous people a lot of money. Leave it to me to get tangled up in a bad situation. *Shocker*.

But, it's what I do. I'm a fuck-up and no one, including myself, ever believed I had much potential to be anything else.

I hop on the Pacific Coast Highway and cruise along the ocean toward Santa Monica. The sun starts to set and the waves crash along the shore. If I had time, I'd pull over and sit for awhile. Just soak it in and smoke a cigarette. But, I have to hop on the freeway and make my way back to the smoggy Valley.

Tonight, the fights take place in Sun Valley, an industrial section of town, a little Northeast of Hollywood. Each week the fights are held at a different location and the audience receives the address only hours before the fighting kicks off.

Like the movie says, the first rule of any fight club is don't talk about it.

There's a cover charge to get in and people place bets on who they think will win. Anyone looking to let off some steam can participate in the bare-knuckle slugfests. The locations are always packed and the illegal fights are three, three-minute rounds. And, there are only three simple rules: no kicking, no biting and no punches below the belt.

Obviously, not much can be done in terms of safety because punching with your bare-knuckles usually causes serious cuts, bleeding and broken jaws. Good thing I'm quick and agile. Maybe I missed my calling as a professional boxer.

After weaving through traffic for about 30 minutes, I find myself cruising past grimy warehouses and factories. It's not a great area, but perfect for the illegal fights. I pull my bike up to the warehouse and check out the crowded parking lot. *Gonna be a big audience tonight. Bigger than usual,* I think.

*Hmm. I wonder why?*

Whatever. I slide my gloves and helmet off and make my way inside. It's loud and the crowd tonight is rambunctious. Already, they look drunk and rowdy. This big of a crowd, I figure my winning take should be around $1,000.

*If* I win.

But, first I have to beat whoever they match me up against. I don't have a choice. At this point, the guys I owe money want to collect and if I don't pay up, I'm going to wind up with a pair of broken arms and legs or dead in a ditch.

Not sure which is better.

Tonight, they have hay bales set up as the ring. I wouldn't be surprised if there are almost 1,000 people here. I guess they're attracted to the danger and mystery of the whole thing. Fight clubs represent rebellion and everything that a civil society considers taboo. And, the truth is, primitive violence is stamped into our genetic codes. Watching someone get their jaw crushed in a bare-knuckle fight is a thrill.

When the announcer appears and walks into the center of the hay bales, a cheer erupts. There's nothing special about him, but he's the one who gets the crowd pumped. Like me, he wears jeans and a t-shirt and riles the room up with a lot of trash talk.

The fights start not long after and a referee decides each winner. I watch the other fighters closely because then if I'm paired up with any of them in the future, I already know their strengths and weaknesses. I have a good memory like that.

I watch match after match and see a lot of injuries occur. A lot of these guys have no skills. They just want to jump into the ring and throw some punches, blow off some steam. At least I can say I've taken some boxing lessons so I don't look like a complete idiot when I'm out there. I know how to stand and position my body. I know how to throw a punch and I definitely know how to dodge one, too.

By the time I'm up, it's the end of the night. I take my jewelry off-- my watch, chunky rings and a couple of beaded and braided leather bracelets-- and shove it all into the pocket of my leather coat. Then, I pull my shirt over my head and toss it onto the nearest hay bale.

I'm not the biggest or thickest guy in the room in terms of muscles, but I'm 6'3" and have a lean, powerful build. I also have a body covered in ink and piercings. And, when I say covered, I mean from my fingers up to the back of my hands, up both my arms and around my torso, front and back. I have a design on the back of my neck, too. You name it, I probably got it inked into my skin at some point-- skull, cross, rose, dice, a checkered racing flag, eagle, anchor, panther and words like "pain," "sinner" and, of course, "Madison."

I have a few less piercings than tattoos, but still a lot compared to the average person. Maybe a bit more risqué, too-- a barbell through both nipples and my ears and cartilage pierced.

It gives me a more dangerous look. Like anyone who would put their body through so much pain is a crazy kind of look and I hope my opponent is intimidated.

When I see my opponent, I'm not overly worried. He's an Asian guy, maybe about 5'8" and, honestly, he doesn't look that tough. But, I've learned to never underestimate anyone. For all I know, the dude knows Krav Maga and will kick my ass.

We step into the ring and I notice the announcer holds a box. *Oh, shit.* It's going to be a fight with weapons. Sometimes, the host of these fights likes to get creative with the violence. Looks like I'll be a part of that tonight whether I like it or not.

The announcer opens the box to reveal two sharp, serrated military-looking knives.

*Oh, for fuck's sake.*

I really don't want to get stabbed tonight, but I have to fight. I push my hair back which is always too long on top, reach into the box and take a knife. *Just keep moving and be quick,* I coach myself. *After three, three-minute rounds, you're done.*

But, in order to win, I'm going to have to inflict some damage. At least one wound.

Then, the bell rings and it's on.

I lift my knife, in a fighting stance, and circle around my opponent. His name's Tiger and it doesn't take me long to realize he's fast. He dances around me like he's had some kind of martial arts training and he wields the knife with confidence.

God, I just want to get this over with and leave.

The cheers escalate and he lunges and slices. I jump back and barely miss getting gutted. *Fucker.* I guess Tiger isn't playing nice tonight. Ten seconds later, I return the favor. I use a fake out, though, dodge left, but really move right and manage to catch his upper arm with the tip of my knife.

The crowd roars and Tiger pins me with a black look.

"C'mon," I goad him and motion with my fingers.

The rounds move lightning-fast. I win round one. In the middle of the second round, he ducks and slashes my lower leg so he wins that one. We enter the final round tied and I need to get this done. I have to get that $1,000 prize or I may as well just let Tiger here stab me in the heart.

I see my chance in the last 30 seconds. He managed to nick the top of my hand early on, but now I'm going for the win. When Tiger drops and slides toward me, aiming for my leg again, I easily sidestep him, spin and slash him across the back.

Done. And, I can thank my long legs for that maneuver.

The referee calls me the winner, yanks my arm up into the air and the crowd goes wild.

I glance over at Tiger and instead of being a gracious loser, he swears at me. At least, I assume he's saying something not nice in his native language. Whatever. I don't care. I just grab my shirt and jacket and go up to collect my winnings.

I walk away with $1200. *Not too bad for a night's work.*

Unfortunately, this isn't the last time I see Tiger and his knife.

# 3

## HARLOW

The party up at Easton's is even more fun than I expect. There's delicious champagne and food, but even better is the group of people that I'm now calling my friends.

The guys are a riot and make me laugh like I haven't laughed in years. Griff, Ryker and Logan Sharpe, Jax's friend from when he used to be on the force, tease Jax relentlessly. But, really, the only true bachelor among them is Logan. Ryker is now married and Griff will be soon enough.

I give the police detective a little glance. He's well over six-feet tall, 35 years old with a head of thick chestnut hair nearly the same shade as mine and shrewd caramel-colored eyes that have a tired, jaded look. I know he works too long, too hard and sees the worst of humanity.

There's no doubt the man is attractive, but he's a little clean-cut for me. I tend to like men who have an edge. Who possesses that dirty-hot look and bad boy attitude. Kind of like Jax. But, Jax is my boss and a married man. I would never look at him in any way other than like a brother.

Then, there's Hottie McHottie himself, the Brad Pitt of our little entourage, Griff. He's so in love with my best friend Lexi and I couldn't be more thrilled. I worked with Griff a few times before we ever actually met when he was still an operative with the CIA. He's how I got the job at P.S.

And, of course, former Navy SEAL Ryker Flynn towers over the entire room at 6'4" and has a huge body composed of solid, rock-hard muscle. Right now, he's whispering something into Avery's ear and I'm sure it's naughty because she blushes and slaps at his arm.

It's nice to see everyone happy and paired up. I talk to Liv, Easton's assistant, for a bit and then wander outside with another glass of bubbly and lean against the glass wall, admiring the view from way up here in the Hollywood Hills.

My mind wanders to work, as usual, and I start to think about all the different cases the guys are working on and all the information they need from me. After I finish my drink, I think I'll stop by the office and work. It's late, but I don't mind. I like going in and feeling useful. I also like being there when it's quiet-- early in the morning or later in the evening-- when I can really concentrate and not get interrupted.

Five minutes later, I set my empty glass down and make my way back inside. I hug everyone goodbye and wish Jax and Easton safe travels on their honeymoon to Greece. It was kind of a last minute decision, but the moment that Easton found out Jax had some Greek heritage and that he'd never been there, she knew they had to go.

"Drinks this weekend, right?" Lexi asks me.

I nod. "Sounds good."

The Uber only takes a few minutes to reach me and then we head down the hill and over to East Hollywood where Platinum Security is located. It doesn't take long to get there and I pull out my key and go inside, flipping on the lights.

I love being here when it's quiet and peaceful. I get so much work done and since business is booming, Jax told me to pick out some new equipment. I am a tech geek at heart and always in the know about the latest gadgets and gizmos. At this point, I'd say my office here has more and better toys than at my apartment.

In my office, I slip out of my dress and into a t-shirt, jeans and boots that I keep stashed here.

Lately, I've been staying away from my place and coming here as much as possible. I don't know what it is, but when I'm there, I get this overwhelming sense of loneliness. It just feels dark and depressing.

I walk into the tiny kitchen, brew some coffee and reach for one of the mugs the guys gifted me. They're a riot and have different sayings on them like "Hacker. My other computer is your computer," "In code we trust" and "Profanity is the most used language in programming."

*What can I say?* The guys get a kick out of how easily I can start swearing. *Like a fucking sailor.* But, that's what happens when you have two older brothers and a father who's nothing but a bad influence.

I tilt the pot and fill my mug. Then, I take a long, satisfied sip. I love my coffee. Live to have a fresh, hot mug of it at any time of the day. Black, of course. All that cream and sugar destroys it for me.

After a fortifying drink of caffeine, I head into my office, boot my computer up and plop down on my throne. I feel like a queen with my three large monitors and various tech equipment. Right away, I feel myself get absorbed into my online searches. I run backdoor programs and wait for results, contact other hackers for possible information and search the Dark Web.

I'm not sure how long I've been working, but I know it's three cups of coffee later when I hear a commotion outside. I tilt my head, listening. The office isn't located in the greatest part of town, but we've never had any trouble here. And, I locked the door so I should be fine.

My fingers fly across my keyboard and I continue to work. *Everything is fine,* I tell myself.

A moment later, there's a string of loud sounds. Yelling, pounding, a cracking noise and finally a low cry.

*Shit.* It sounds like the glass front door broke. Okay, everything is *not* fine.

I pull my glasses off, jump up and wish to God that one of the guys was here. They always carry a gun and right about now, I wish I did, too. I take a deep, steadying breath and peek out into the hallway.

And, the first thing I see is a body slumped against the broken front door.

*Are you fucking kidding me?*

Maybe he got jumped. I don't know, but I hurry forward to see if he needs help. Before I unlock the door, I glance out, but don't see anyone else. Just a man in a black leather jacket on the ground, laying against the door.

I turn the bolt and when I pull the door inward, the man falls backwards and sprawls into the entranceway. Laying on his back, he looks up at me with the most intriguing shade of hazel eyes I've ever seen. The hallway light shines down, highlighting them perfectly, and they're sage green threaded in gold, rimmed in long black lashes that any woman would die to have.

"You have freckles," he says in a low voice.

*What?* I blink, at a loss for words, wondering why he seems familiar. There's something about him...

Then, I see he's clutching his side and my eyes widen. "Oh, my God, you're bleeding." I drop down and push his long fingers aside. His t-shirt is torn and blood soaks through. I pull the edge of the shirt up to get a better look at how badly he's hurt and get an eyeful of ink. Damn, he's tatted up like crazy.

"What happened?" I ask, pulling my gaze away from his endless ink and back up to his amazing eyes.

"Got stabbed," he murmurs, staring up at me.

"No shit," I say. God, his eyes are mesmerizing. He's also sporting some piercings which I like.

"Call Jax," he says.

*He knows Jax? Who the hell is this?*

Then, he mumbles something else and I lean closer, trying to make out what he's saying. "You're even prettier up close."

My stomach somersaults.

And, then he passes out.

For a moment, I sit there, but then I snap into action. I stand up, reach under his arms and drag him all the way into the office. *God, he's heavy*. With a grunt, I clear his long-ass legs over the threshold and close the front door, locking it. Then, I run down to the tiny kitchen, find a clean towel and return.

I also grab my cell phone and, as I drop down to apply pressure to his wound, I dial Jax. I hate to bother him, but obviously they know each other.

"Jax Wilder," he answers.

"It's Harlow," I say. "I'm sorry to bother you, but I'm at the office and there was a fight or something outside. Someone got stabbed and he's in here now. Asking for you."

*"What?"*

"Yeah. I don't know who he is, but-"

"I'm on my way."

I let out a breath and look down at the unconscious man. Damn, he's attractive. The tattoos, the piercings, the leather jacket...the stab wound. Everything about him screams bad boy and that's right up my alley.

My gaze roams over his tan face. He has thick dark eyebrows, a scar below his right eye that sits high up on his cheekbone and a nose with a slight bump in its center which makes me think it's been broken once or twice. Dark scruff covers his jaw and his brown hair, longer on top and shorter on the sides, looks lighter under the fluorescent bulbs and streaked with gold.

Actually, his haircut reminds me a lot of Jax's.

I check the towel and it looks like the bleeding finally stopped. Still, I keep pressure on the wound. It's right at his side, above his hip bone, and I let my eyes wander over some of the tattoos there. Right below his navel, there's an eagle and an anchor and...an "X" right above the button of his jeans. *As in "X" marks the spot?* I wonder. *Oh, God.*

I pull my gaze back up, admiring his slim build and the way his hip bones jut out. I'd be willing to bet he has a six-pack, but his shirt covers his abs. Temptation makes me move my hand off the towel and slide his shirt up just a bit higher.

Yep, six-pack galore.

Suddenly, the lock clicks open and I snap my hand back, guilt making my cheeks flush. Jax throws the cracked glass door open and his dark eyes widen before he drops down on the other side of the man.

"Sebastian?" he says and yanks the towel off, checking out the wound. "It's just a nick." He lets out a relieved breath.

*Sebastian?* His brother! No wonder he seemed familiar.

"What the fuck?" Jax shakes his head. "Let's move him onto the couch."

With a nod, I jump up and open the door to Jax's office. Jax lifts his brother beneath the arms and moves him much easier and more quickly than I did.

A moment later, he lays Sebastian out on the couch and then pulls a first aid kit from his bottom desk drawer. Sebastian moans and Jax helps him out of the leather jacket and then pulls the bloody shirt off.

And, I get a really good look at those ridges in his perfect abs. *Damn.* I feel my heart skip a beat as I ogle Jax's brother, laid out on the couch, shirtless, barbells through his nipples, inked and only in a pair of worn jeans that sit low on his hips. Like *really* low.

I swallow hard and watch Jax clean the cut. Again, Sebastian moans. Then, those long lashes flutter open and I can see his beautiful hazel eyes again.

"Stings," he mumbles.

Jax deliberately pours more alcohol over the wound and Sebastian hisses. "What the fuck, Bastian?" Jax grumbles.

"Congrats," Bastian says. "You've got yourself a beautiful wife."

Jax stops swabbing the cut and raises a dark brow. "How would you know?"

"Couldn't miss my big brother's wedding. I watched from behind a tree."

Jax lets out a breath and shakes his head. "You should've been there in the front row. And, at the reception."

"Didn't want to mess up your day. But, guess I managed to do that, anyway." An apology flashes in his hazel eyes.

"Christ, Bastian. I want you around. Where have you been this past year?"

But, he only shakes his head and tries to make a joke out of the situation. "Oh, you know. Just up to my usual shenanigans."

"I'm serious," Jax says and secures a bandage over the clean wound. "I fuckin' miss you, idiot." He lightly slaps his younger brother upside the head.

"Missed you, too," Bastian says.

I look from Jax to Bastian and, after their little moment, I clear my throat. "I'm Harlow, by the way," I say.

Bastian's gorgeous hazel eyes flick in my direction and my stomach somersaults.

# 4

# BASTIAN

H*arlow.* I like her name. I like her long dark hair. I like her breathy voice and I especially like the dusting of freckles across the bridge of her nose.

"Shit, sorry, Harlow," Jax says. "This is my brother Sebastian."

"Call me Bastian," I say and struggle to sit up straighter.

"So, who stabbed you this time?" Jax asks, his tone dry.

I shrug. I don't want to drag Jax down into my shit so it's better if I just make sure he stays uninvolved. "Random attack. I think they wanted…" I finally remember the $1200 that was in my pocket. My prize money and payment to Angelo. I grab my jacket, shove my hand into the pocket and realize it's gone. *Goddammit.* My eyes slide shut. *Now what am I going to do?*

"Wanted what?" Jax asks.

"My watch," I say lamely.

But, Jax isn't stupid and I know he doesn't believe me.

After the fight, I decided to ride by here because I had heard about Jax opening an office. I didn't expect Tiger and his entourage to follow me over here and continue our knife fight. But, that's exactly what happened and before I knew it, the three of them had me up against the door.

One of them slammed me against the front door and it cracked the glass. Then, Tiger swooped in and stuck his blade in my side. I dropped and that's when they must've taken the prize money. *Fuckers.*

Suddenly, Jax's cell phone rings. He stands up, pulls it out of his pocket and his face softens. "Hey, Princess," he says. "Long story. I'll tell you when I get back. Yeah, I know. I'll hurry. Bye, baby."

Jax turns, glances down at his watch. "Our flight leaves in less than two hours. I have to go or Easton will kill me."

"Your honeymoon?" I ask and he nods. "Go, shit, I don't wanna keep you."

"Easton wants to meet you. She's going to be pissed you hid behind a tree today."

"When you get back," I say.

"Will you still be here?" Jax asks. "Or, are you planning to run away again?"

"I'll wait till you get back. I just need to find a place to stay."

"You can stay at my apartment," Jax says. "For as long as you want. Next week I'm moving into Easton's place permanently." He looks at his watch again. "I don't have time to drive you there now, but..."

"I've got my bike," I say.

"No. You're injured."

"I can take him," Harlow offers.

I glance over and she offers me a tentative smile. I look at her, a moment too long, feeling the pull of her blue-gray eyes.

"Thanks, Harlow. Take the company car," Jax says. Then, he focuses on me, narrowing his eyes. "If you jet while I'm gone, I'm going to hunt you down and kick your sorry ass."

"I won't," I promise. "Just go and enjoy your honeymoon. I'll be here when you get back."

With a nod, Jax hands me the key to his apartment. "Be back in a week. Try not to burn the place down."

"Have fun," I say. Jax gives a nod and is about to turn away. But, then, he lays a hand on my shoulder and, in a low voice, says, "I'm glad you were there today, bro."

"Me, too," I say.

After another nod, Jax walks out and I find myself alone with Harlow. I liked her dress earlier, but now I like her in the snug t-shirt and fitted denim much better. I drag my gaze away and pull myself up off the couch. I hiss in a breath and touch my side.

"Are you okay?" she asks.

"I'll be fine," I say and carefully slip into my leather jacket.

"Ready?" she asks.

When I nod, she takes a set of car keys off Jax's desk and grabs her laptop as we head out. The company car, a brand new, black Range Rover, sits at the curb and she unlocks it. *Guess business is good.* I slip into the passenger side, adjust my seat all the way back so I can stretch my legs and watch her pull the safety belt over her lap and start the car.

"Jax's place is close," she says.

"That's too bad," I drawl, studying her profile.

"Why?" she asks.

"It's not too often I get chauffeured around by a beautiful woman."

Even though it's dark, I think she blushes. "Aren't you the charmer?"

"Just being honest."

We drive down the main road for a minute and then she turns onto a side street. Harlow pulls up alongside the curb and puts the SUV in park. Then, she turns to me. "You really have no idea who attacked you?" she asks.

I don't say anything. Just shrug.

"Because I could help you find out."

"How?" I ask and frown.

"I can check the security footage of any nearby cameras."

"You're a hacker?" I ask. *Impressive.*

"Let's just say I'm good with computers."

I bet she's good with other things, too. My gaze drops to her full lips and I get the urge to kiss her. Instead, I run a hand through my hair. I know who stabbed me, but, dammit, I really want to spend some more time with her. "Okay, sure."

Harlow turns the car off and we head up the walkway to Jax's apartment. "Number 12," she says.

"My lucky number," I say.

She looks up, levels that steel blue gaze on me and her mouth edges up. "Mine, too."

As she unlocks the door, I slant her a look. "So, you and my brother…" I don't ask if there's history there, but I let the question hang in the air. And, as I wait for her to confirm or deny, I wish with my entire being that their relationship is, and always was, completely platonic.

"Jax is my boss," she says and pushes the door open. "I've worked for him a couple of months and I've never seen a man so in love with a woman like he is with Easton."

*Hmm.* Something warm passes through me and, all of a sudden, I'm very curious about Miss Harlow-

"What's your last name?" I ask out of the blue.

"Vaughn," she answers.

Harlow Vaughn. *Yeah, I like it. I like it a lot.*

*I like her a lot.*

Jax's place is small and simple, but perfect for me. I don't need anything fancy and I'm grateful to have a roof over my head. I wander around, checking it out, and wind up in the kitchen. I open the fridge and see it's stocked with beer and champagne. "I take it, Easton must like champagne?"

Harlow walks up behind me and glances into the fridge. "Oh, yeah," she says with a chuckle. "And, it's the expensive stuff."

I pull a bottle out and find two glasses. "Join me?"

There's a brief hesitation, but then she smiles. "Why not?"

I pop the cork, fill both glasses and hand her one. "To you," I say and clink my glass against hers. "Thank you for rescuing me tonight, Miss Vaughn."

She laughs and takes a sip. "Glad I could be of service."

A couple of dirty thoughts run through my head. *Because, yeah, I'd definitely like Harlow to service me.*

# 5

## HARLOW

I study Bastian over the rim of my glass and feel a tingle run through me. There's something about him that draws me in like I'm metal and he's a magnet. It's an attraction like I've never experienced before and, against my better judgement, I want to explore it.

I've never met anyone quite like him and he's beginning to fascinate me. But, I'm not stupid. Sebastian Wilder is bad news. There's a dangerous, sharp edge to him and I know if I get too close, he'd cut me. He's wild and charismatic and I'm sure he has no shortage of bed partners when he wants one.

But, he's not the type to commit. Sure, he may rock your world all night, but the moment the sun begins to rise, he will kick you to the curb. I know his type and understand that what you see is what you get.

Bastian meets my gaze and his mouth edges up. I like his smile. It softens him, reminds me that under that tough, rebel exterior, he's just a man. Apparently, a man who doesn't like to stay in the same place too long.

"So," I say and head over to the couch and my laptop. "I'm surprised I haven't met you before."

Bastian follows me, carrying the bottle of champagne over, and sits down next to me. He refills my glass and stretches those long legs out. "I've been away this past year," he says.

"Where?" I ask and open my computer.

"Oh, you know. Just here and there." He gives me a lazy, Cheshire cat smile.

"I didn't think you and Jax were close, but...it just looked like you were or, at least used to be."

"We've always been close," Bastian says. "I just don't want him to worry about me."

"Why would he worry about you?"

"How about we talk about something else?" He picks up my glass and hands it to me. "You stopped drinking."

I take the glass and our fingers brush. And, it's fucking electric. I suck in a quick breath not expecting his touch to have such a jolting effect on me. I take a long sip. "I had a few glasses at Easton's earlier. I probably shouldn't be drinking more."

"Why not?"

"Because I don't drink all that much. Especially champagne. It kind of goes straight to my head," I admit with a giggle.

Oh, my God, did I just *giggle*? How embarrassing. He probably thinks I'm flirting with him.

He gives me another lazy smile. "Drink up. You're safe with me."

"Promise you won't take advantage?" The minute the words are out of my mouth, I regret them. *Stop flirting with him, Harlow.* He is a huge complication that you do not need in your life. And, the fact that he's Jax's brother makes it worse.

Those hazel eyes pierce me like a dagger. "Jax would kill me."

"Jax isn't here," I say and take another sip. *Shit, I need to stop.* I set my glass down, vowing not to drink anymore. But, I see my glass and the bottle are both empty. *Oops.*

"Are you drunk?" he asks.

I shake my head. "Just a little tipsy." I hiccup and cover my mouth.

Bastian chuckles. "I think you're more than tipsy, freckles."

I scrunch my nose up. "Ugh, don't remind me." When he raises a brow, I point to my nose. "I hate my freckles."

He makes a face. "Why? They're hot."

I burst out laughing. "Freckles are *not* hot."

"I like yours."

I feel my cheeks grow warm and glance away, suddenly shy. When he sits up, his leather jacket falls open and I'm reminded that he isn't wearing a shirt underneath. I bite my lip and my gaze automatically slides down his bare chest and abs. *Damn.* He is way too hot and beyond dangerous.

*Time to go,* I tell myself. But, I couldn't pry myself up off this couch for a thousand bucks. For a million bucks. I lick my lips and his green-gold gaze drops.

Something ignites between us. The cushion beneath me dips as he moves closer and I breathe his scent in for the first time. *Good God.* His skin smells delicious. Sensual like some kind of caramelized copper with a tang of salty herbs. Earthy and masculine. The human equivalent of crystal meth. I don't know if it's his natural smell or some faded cologne he dabbed on earlier, but all I know is it's really, really sexy.

When Bastian lifts his hands and cups them around my face, I feel my stomach drop away. His hazel eyes hold mine for a moment before he slants his head and captures my mouth. There's nothing soft or gentle about it. It's all heat and pressure and chemistry like I've never felt before. His mouth opens, deepening the kiss and his tongue glides past my lips.

Our tongues meet and circle, wary at first, then more bold. He tastes like expensive champagne and my hands slip inside his jacket, skimming up his naked chest as if they have a mind of their own. His skin is so warm and I feel a shiver run through my whole body.

Sensation overwhelms me and my fingers toy with the bars in his pierced nipples. When I tug them, he groans into my mouth and his hands leave my face and slide up into my hair. His long fingers twine through the strands near my scalp and he pulls hard. Not hard enough to hurt, but good enough to rip a moan from my throat.

"You like that?" he asks.

"Hell yeah," I say and lean into his bare chest.

When his lips drop and kiss down the curve of my neck, I feel a tingle all the way down to my toes.

"I think you and I are a lot alike," Bastian whispers, scraping his teeth along the sensitive skin and then he nips my neck.

I feel like I'm caught in some kind of trance, unable to escape. And, I don't even care. I slide his jacket off and look down. His inked chest rises and falls with deep, slightly uneven breaths and I trail a finger along the word "Madison" written over his heart.

His sister who died a year ago.

I lift my eyes to his, but he doesn't offer any explanation. Just dips his head and takes my lips again. How the kiss could possibly be hotter than before, I don't know. But, it is and I let out a soft, little whimper as his mouth devours mine.

Bastian kisses me like a man who is half feral and on the prowl.

He pushes me back into the couch, moving over me, and I reach up and pull him down. One of his hands rests on my hip and the other slides up over the curve of my breast. I arch up into his palm, feeling better than I've felt in years.

I know I'm being reckless, but I blame it on being alone for so damn long. Because of my self-imposed isolation. And, a little on the excessive champagne. But, even if I were dead sober, I'd still want this man.

Because he is offering me something that I've been missing my whole life. I can't exactly even say what. All I know is I'm feeling things I've never experienced before and my mind and body want to succumb.

And, then his phone rings. *Shit.*

He pulls back, reaches for his jacket and shoves a hand into the pocket. I see him roll his eyes. "Jax," he tells me and slides the bar over to answer. "Hey, big brother."

I sit up and straighten my t-shirt. Maybe it's a good thing Jax called. Things were starting to move a little fast and having a one-night stand with Sebastian Wilder is not the smartest thing. I need to cool off.

I get up and go into the kitchen. I can feel Bastian's eyes on me as I walk over to the fridge. Leave it to Jax to have no bottled water. I turn to the sink, lean down and gulp a mouthful of cold water from the faucet.

"Yeah, everything's good."

I wipe my face with the back of my hand and turn to lean against the sink, trying to get my legs to stop shaking. Bastian watches me closely with glowing green-gold eyes.

"Um, yeah, she's still here."

*Oh, God.* The last thing I want is for my boss to know that I just downed a bottle of his fiancée's champagne and made out with his brother. I take a deep breath and walk back over, scoop up my laptop, and get ready to leave.

Bastian grabs my wrist. "Hang on," he tells Jax. "You're leaving?" He pins me with a questioning stare.

I nod. "Yeah, it's late."

"Bastian!" Jax yells through the phone line.

"Fuck, hang on," he snaps at Jax. Then, he gets up and moves closer, hazel eyes wide. "What about helping me track down my attacker?"

"I can pull the footage when I get home." I look down at his long fingers clasped around my wrist.

"Gimme a sec. Please," he adds and lets go.

I know I shouldn't, but I nod.

Bastian lifts the phone back up and must be getting an earful from Jax because he drops his head back and stifles a groan of annoyance. A few minutes later, he finally gets a word in and mumbles, "I know. I said, I know. Jesus. Don't worry about it and just have a good honeymoon." He hangs up. "Sorry. My brother can be a pain in the ass."

"I should go," I say and turn toward the door.

"Harlow-"

"I can email you the footage," I tell him and open the door. When I turn, his gaze is inscrutable, but he nods.

"Sure," he finally says. "But, you don't have my email."

He's right. Bastian grabs his phone and pulls his contacts up. "What's your number?" he asks.

And, like an idiot, I tell him. Then, I bolt.

# 6

## BASTIAN

G*ood job, idiot.* Way to make her run, I tell myself.

And, talk about impeccable timing. *Thanks a lot, Jax.* If he hadn't called then I can only imagine what would've happened. What we would be doing right now. My groin tightens at the thought and the memory of kissing and touching Harlow.

Harlow Vaughn is exactly what I like in a woman. She's fearless, strong and I'm willing to bet an absolute wild cat in the sack. And, she smells like strawberries.

I fucking *love* strawberries.

Everything seemed to be going really well for a minute there. Then, she freaked out. I don't know if it's because she didn't want Jax to know she was here still or because her buzz was wearing off. Doesn't really matter, though, because she couldn't get away from me fast enough.

I shove a hand through my hair and curse. *It's probably for the best,* I tell myself. Though, my cock wholeheartedly disagrees.

Other than a night of passion, I have nothing to offer her. Harlow is a smart girl so she must've realized that I'm a dead-end. With a sigh, I pull my jacket on and wince at the wound on my side. Then, I grab a beer from the fridge and go outside.

The night is cool since it's December. But, California-cool means the low sixties. I sit on the front steps, reach into my pocket and pull out my cigarettes. I shake one out, put it between my lips and pop the beer open.

As I light up, I can't stop thinking about Harlow. Kissing her was like...shit, I can't even think of a strong enough comparison. I inhale, filling my lungs with smoke, and then lean my head back and exhale. Above me, the stars shine brightly and the moon is nearly full. Maybe that explains my crazy behavior tonight. Chalk it up to the full moon.

I know that's not it, though. It's what I told her: *I think you and I are a lot alike.*

It's strange, but I feel like we're kindred spirits or something. Like she actually understands me. And, she sure as hell isn't intimidated by the way I look. God, when we were kissing, I thought she was going to yank my barbell piercings right out.

But, I liked it. She has a confidence and passion about her that turns me on. Like hardcore, I think, and take a sip of the beer.

It's too damn bad this can't go anywhere, though. I can already tell that Jax would have a cow and that alone wouldn't stop me. But, right now, I have other things to deal with-- like finding the money to pay Angelo back.

Angelo Savini runs a local bookie operation, among other illegal things, and I made a few too many bets and lost. Now, I owe him around ten grand and he's tired of waiting.

I always seem to find myself in dire situations like this. In trouble with people who I should go out of my way to avoid. But, no, that's not me. I'm drawn to trouble and ways I can make a quick buck. Unfortunately, it tends to backfire in my face more often than not.

When my phone rings, my hackles raise in irritation. *Just get on the damn plane, Jax.* I yank my cell out and I'm about to yell those words into the phone, but then see "Unknown Caller" on the i.d.

"Yeah," I say.

"Mr. Wilder, I'd like to talk to you about the money you owe me."

*Shit.* "Angelo, funny you're calling because I had partial payment-"

"I don't want partial payment, Bastian. I want the full ten grand now. Can you pay it or not?"

"If you give me a few days-"

"So, no. That's what I figured you'd say so I've come up with an alternative way you can pay off your debt."

"What?" I ask in a wary voice.

"A simple job."

I wait for him to give me more details, but I already have a feeling I'm not going to like it. A "simple job" for Angelo Savini could be anything from a drug deal to murder. I feel my stomach clench.

"All you need to do is make sure someone is at a specific location at a designated time."

A frown creases my brow. That sounds a little too easy and a warning bell goes off in my head. Not that I ever heed it, though.

"There's a woman who works at your brother's security firm-- a hacker named Harlow Vaughn. I have a few questions for her."

*Fuck.* My heart sinks.

"She has access to information I need. You bring her to me and your debt is settled."

"What kind of information?" I ask.

"That's none of your concern," Angelo says. "Your job is to get the girl to the specified location and that's it. Couldn't be more simple, Bastian. Even a loser like you can't fuck it up."

I want to tell this asshole to go to hell, but clamp my teeth together and weigh my options. Lure Harlow somewhere so he can talk to her or wind up in a ditch?

Really not much of a choice on my part. But, I don't want him to hurt her.

"You're just going to ask her some questions?"

"That's it," he says easily, but somehow I don't feel any reassurance at the quick response.

"And, then let her leave?"

"Exactly."

My mind races. Harlow is a talented hacker from what I know so maybe he wants her to dig up some information about somebody.

Probably one of his enemies or rivals. If she didn't do questionable shit online then Angelo probably wouldn't have any interest in her or need those shady skills of hers.

This is kind of her fault, I reason. If she played it straight then this wouldn't be happening. Hell, the same goes for me. I feel stuck between a rock and a hard place for about 10 seconds. Then, I make my decision.

"And, you'll forget the entire ten grand?" I confirm.

"Completely forgiven. Do we have a deal, Mr. Wilder?"

"Yeah," I say. "We have a deal."

"Wonderful. I'll be in touch with further details when it's time."

Angelo hangs up and I stuff my phone back into my pocket. I take one last drag of the cigarette and then stub it out against the cement step.

What information does Harlow have that Angelo wants? I wonder.

He said it's going to be a few questions and then she's free to go. But, why does a part of me not fully believe him? The idea of handing her over to a guy like Angelo leaves a bad taste in my mouth. I know he just got out of prison a month or so ago, but like me, he doesn't learn his lesson.

Why am I thinking so hard about this? It's not like he's going to rape and torture her.

Right?

*Shit.* What choice do I have? If I don't take her to him, I'm going to wind up gutted or chopped up into little pieces.

And, I'd rather that didn't happen.

I might be a screw-up and a hot mess, but one thing about me is consistent and true. And, the reason why women, especially Harlow Vaughn, should stay far, far away.

Because I'm a selfish asshole.

So, if delivering a woman I barely know to Angelo Savini will get me back in his good graces then what the hell? I don't owe her anything.

But, I owe Angelo quite a bit.

# 7

# HARLOW

Early the next morning, I suck down endless cups of coffee and try not to think about how I made out with my boss's younger brother. My head hurts from too many glasses of champagne, but I remember everything that happened quite clearly.

And, honestly, it would probably be better if I didn't. If it were just a hazy, alcohol-induced memory that I could forget all about.

But, no. I remember every detail with crystal clarity and I can't seem to stop obsessing over Bastian Wilder. I can still feel the way his lips moved over mine and the silky glide of his tongue in my mouth and along my neck. The bite on my neck that left a little red mark. That deep guttural groan of his when I toyed with the barbell piercings. And, how when I got home and changed, my panties were soaked.

*Dammit.* What am I going to do?

My sensible side is warning me to stay far away from him. But, I'm dawn to his darkness, that wild side of him that no one will ever be able to tame. I understand him. I hate to admit it, but he's a lot like my Dad. They both love trouble and the quick payoff. They're irresponsible, incorrigible and possess this innate magnetism that can't be denied.

For the first time since I can remember, I can't concentrate on work. With a sigh, I push my chair back and frown. A moment later, I hear Griff and Ryker walk into the office. They head right to my office and stroll inside.

"What the hell happened to the front door?" Griff asks. "And, of course, it happened on my watch. Because don't forget, kids, I'm in charge while Jax is off honeymooning."

"Morning, Harlow," Ryker says and sets a fresh cup of coffee on my desk. "And, would you shut it already? We know you're in charge, 007."

"Thanks," I say and reach for the large styrofoam cup. I probably shouldn't drink it because I have the caffeine jitters, but I don't care. After a long satisfying sip, I force a smile. "The broken front door is courtesy of Sebastian Wilder."

Griff arches a brow and sits on the edge of my desk. "Bastian's in town?"

"Yes. I met him last night after someone threw him against the door and stabbed him."

"What?" Griff exclaims.

Ryker crosses his arms. "So, he's here and skipped the wedding?"

"No, apparently he was there, hiding behind a tree or something."

"Jax knows all this, right?" Griff asks.

"Yeah. I called him after I found Bastian out on the sidewalk. I had no idea who he was and Jax came right over."

"Thank God," Griff says. "Because I would not want to call him right now and tell him any of this."

"I bet he was pissed," Ryker says.

"Actually, I think he was just happy to see his brother. And, that he was at the wedding even if it was from afar."

"So who stabbed him? He's okay, right?"

"He says he doesn't know. That it was random. But, yeah, he's fine."

Griff and Ryker exchange a look. Like they're not buying it.

"What?" I get the feeling they know more about Bastian than I do. And, I want to know more details. The nitty-gritty.

"Well, Bastian is..." Griff's voice trails off and he looks to Ryker.

"A fucking pain in the ass," Ryker finishes.

"I was trying to come up with a more politically-correct term, but yeah, he's a pain in the ass. Jax's ass to be more specific."

"I didn't get that impression," I say, coming to his defense. "I mean he's definitely a bit of a troublemaker maybe-"

They burst out laughing. "Just a bit," Griff says.

"Tell me," I say and look from one to the other.

"He's just all about himself and always involved in some kind of shady shit. Jax had to bail him out of trouble a few different times."

"The kid just never learns his lesson," Ryker adds.

"And, then he fucking disappears. Maybe if he hung around all of us a little more, he'd make some better choices with his life."

Now, it's my turn to laugh. "Oh, yeah. Because you three are all shining examples of perfection."

"That's not what I'm saying. But, we have had some help getting our lives back together. Thanks to some lovely ladies," he adds with a grin.

"Bastian could definitely use a good woman to help him get his life back on track," Ryker says. "The kid's a hot mess. He's going to wind up six-feet under after he screws the wrong person. Or, give poor Jax a heart attack."

*Yeah, especially if he finds out what happened between us,* I think. And, I don't want to be responsible for killing Easton's husband.

"I don't know. I think you guys are being a little harsh. Bastian seems nice."

Griff and Ryker exchange another look.

"Harlow," Griff says carefully, "Bastian is a lot of things, but don't be fooled. He's all about himself."

I look from one to the other and lean back in my chair. "Couldn't we say the same thing about you a few months ago? Before you met Lexi?"

Griff's bright blue eyes narrow. "Fucking A. You *like* him."

*Dammit.* Griff Lawson is too perceptive. Or, am I just that transparent? For a moment, I don't admit or deny it. But, they're waiting for me to say something so I just force out a laugh. "Don't be silly. I just offered to help him out and pull some footage from nearby cameras. Maybe identify his attacker."

My phone buzzes with a text and I glance down. It's Bastian. Oh, God, what can he possibly want? I'm dying to open it and find out, but need to get rid of these two first.

"Look, I appreciate the concern, but I can take care of myself," I tell them.

"That him?" Griff asks, eyeing my phone.

"What? No." I shake my head and flip my phone over. God, he's uncanny when it comes to reading people. I guess that's why he made such a good CIA operative.

"He's still in town?"

"He's staying at Jax's apartment."

"You're not going to see him again, are you?"

"Oh, my God, stop interrogating me like I'm some suspect."

"We're just concerned, Harlow," Ryker says. "You're obviously free to see whoever you want." He gives Griff a look that tells him to back off and I appreciate it. I'm a grown woman and can make my own decisions.

"Thanks," I mumble. I glance down at my phone. "I think I'm going to take lunch. I'll see you guys later." I grab my purse and skirt around the two big alpha males in my way. I know they're just looking out for me, but really.

The last thing I need is two more Dads. One is quite enough.

The second I hit the sidewalk, I open the text from Bastian: *Lunch?*

Okay, I know I said I should stay away from him, but what's wrong with meeting him for a meal in a public place? It's not even dinner. Lunch is casual so it's not like a date and there won't be any alcohol involved.

*Sure,* I text back. I pull out my lip gloss and glide some on then reach back and pull my long ponytail over a shoulder. I'm not exactly as dressed up as I was yesterday for the wedding and I rarely wear much more than mascara and lip gloss.

I hope he isn't disappointed. Actually, it would be better if he is, I tell myself. Maybe he wants a more glamorous and stylish woman. Not a dud like me.

Yeah, no, I didn't get that impression. I think Bastian would veer away from high-maintenance women and be more attracted to someone who doesn't come with a lot of drama. A woman who is independent and doesn't require constant pampering, attention and gifts.

Jax's place is close and we meet halfway at a little neighborhood cafe. The walk is quick and easy and I take a deep breath before pushing the cafe door open. He's already there and looks even taller than I remember. My heart skips a beat when he turns and gives me a crooked smile.

"Hey, freckles," he says in a low voice.

Warmth fills me and I try to ignore the flutter in my belly. "Hi," I say.

"Want to eat on the patio?"

"Sure." We walk up to the counter, place our orders and then head out to the back area and find a quiet spot under an umbrella.

I sit down across from Bastian and my gaze goes straight to his tattooed forearms that lay on the tabletop, then the chunky skull ring on his finger and the couple of braided leather bracelets on his thick wrist.

"How're you feeling?" he asks.

I pull my eyes away and look up at him. And, damn, those hazel eyes of his glow a warm green-gold that just makes me want to drown in their depths. "Fine. Why?"

"So, no hangover then?" he asks with a smirk.

I shake my head and let out a low breath. Maybe this wasn't such a good idea. I don't know how it's possible, but he's even more attractive today than he was last night.

*How the hell is that even possible,* I wonder?

# 8

# BASTIAN

I can feel her trying to keep her distance, throwing up walls, and that's not good. I need Harlow to trust me. Completely.

Time to get under her skin, make her comfortable.

*So, then you can throw her to the wolves,* I think. *God, I really am a bastard.*

"I was able to find some footage of the guys who attacked you," she says. "I made a copy of it in case you wanted to go to the police."

I automatically reach down and touch the bandage under my shirt. "Thanks, but I think it was just the wrong place at the wrong time kind of thing. Besides, my side feels much better. Thanks to you," I add under my breath.

A blush heats her cheeks and she reaches for her water. I watch her take a sip and notice things about her that I have never noticed about anyone else before. Like the way her slim fingers curve around the glass. And, how she swirls the straw in the ice each time before she takes a sip. And, my favorite part is the way her tongue pokes out just before her glossy lips wrap around the straw and suck, her cheeks hollowing just a bit.

I give my head a shake and try to focus on something other than the image of Harlow down on her knees, that glossy mouth wrapped around my cock. My hand clenches into a fist and I'm glad the table covers my lap right now because things are getting slightly uncomfortable.

She's saying something, but I have no idea what. "Sorry," I say and pull my gaze up to her steel blue eyes.

"I asked what you do. You know, for a job?"

"Oh, um, I dabble in a lot of different things." *Wow,* I think, *that sounds lame. Even for me.* I may as well have said I don't have a real job and rely on fighting, gambling and hustling to get by. Oh, and I also mooch off my big brother from time to time. When I'm especially down on my luck.

*Shit. I am a complete loser.* Why is someone as smart and beautiful as Harlow wasting her time with me?

"Like what?" she asks.

A server swings by our table and drops off the sandwiches we ordered. Suddenly, I don't feel that hungry. I feel...pathetic. Not good enough for the woman who sits across from me.

"Trust me. You really don't wanna hear my story," I say and shake some ketchup on my fries.

"Yeah, I really do," she says.

I grab a fry and take a bite. "Honestly, there's not much to tell. I move around a lot and prefer it that way."

"Ever think about staying here and maybe working with Jax?"

Work with Harlow in the same office? *Yeah, right.* I shake my head. "Nah. I like to come and go whenever I want. I hate feeling tied down."

Something flashes in her eyes. *Yeah, that's right, freckles. I am not marriage material in any way, shape or form.* Not that she'd be interested, I tell myself.

Harlow swallows a bite of her grilled cheese sandwich and eyes me closely. "You aren't going to tell me anything are you?"

"What? I'm telling you stuff."

"I'm not interested in your generic answers," she says and eats a fry.

I've never had a woman call me out on my bullshit before. It's kind of refreshing. But, that doesn't mean I'm telling her anything. "Okay, well what about you?"

"What about me?"

"How did you become a hacker?"

She reaches for the end of her ponytail and twists the dark brown hair around her hand, thinking for a moment. "I guess my computer was the only one there for me when things got rough." I wait for her to continue. "My parents got divorced, my Mom cried all the time and couldn't deal with my Dad leaving and my older brothers got the hell out and joined the military. I used to hide in my room and spend all day online. And, I learned that you could do anything-- play games, make friends, find information, create programs, break into people's accounts. Steal money, steal identities. I suppose it was my way of rebelling."

"That's impressive. I can barely figure out how to check my email."

Harlow laughs and it makes me smile. "Well, if you ever need any tech support, you know who to contact."

I nod and it occurs to me that I'm not winning any points by giving her evasive answers. A trustworthy guy is going to confide in her and share things. I don't really have any intention of sharing any deep dark secrets, but I need to open up more.

But, small talk really isn't my forte. I'm much better at other things. And, then it hits me. I think the best way for me to gain her trust is to sleep with her. And, let's face it, fucking Harlow Vaughn has been on my mind since I saw her at the wedding yesterday. Not only would it scratch the itch, but also it would help secure her confidence in me.

"What are you doing tonight?" I ask. A plan starts forming in my head about the best way to do this. I don't want to scare her off. I want her to feel comfortable with me. Secure. Trusting. *So then you can fuck her over.*

"I'm working late. With Jax gone, we're really swamped."

"Oh. Well, with all that champagne in my fridge, I thought you might want to come over and have a drink."

Her gaze turns cool and I realize I just screwed up. Way too forward.

"That's okay," she says. "I think I had enough last night."

*Enough champagne?* I wonder. *Or, enough of me?*

I don't know what's happening, but all of my usual charm is gone. Nothing I'm saying is coming out right and I feel like an idiot. *So typical Bastian.* If there's a way to screw it up, you can count on me to do exactly that.

"Sorry," I say. "I didn't mean to sound creepy because that sounded really fucking creepy, didn't it?"

"Kind of sleazy, actually," she admits. But, the twinkle in her eyes is back.

I shake my head and feel my mouth edge up. "I usually come off as a little more charming than this. But...you twist me all up and I can't seem to find the right words." *There. There's some damn honesty.*

Something in her seems to shift and her eyes lower to my left hand which rests on the table.

"What do the numbers mean? Above your knuckles?"

I look down at the black ink. *1222.* And, my heart aches. I don't talk about my tattoos with anyone. I have a lot of them and every single one has meaning. A reason for being. I'm not just some idiot who picks out meaningless shit to get inked on his body forever or to look tough.

For some strange reason, I tell her. "It's the day my parents died in a car accident. December 22." I lift my other hand and flash the numbers inked there as well, also above my knuckles. *0707.* "The day my sister died."

"I'm so sorry," she says in a low voice.

God, I miss them. A wave of sadness washes over me, but then I push it away. If I've learned anything it's that life goes on. You can cry and carry on and mourn, but when the ones you love die, they aren't coming back.

I give a sharp nod.

"I'm glad you invited me to lunch."

I look up and feel myself get sucked up into her blue-gray eyes. "Me, too."

# 9

## HARLOW

After lunch, I stand on the sidewalk with Bastian. The office is to the left and Jax's apartment is to the right so here's where we go our separate ways.

"Thanks for the lunch," I say.

"Thanks for coming."

"Guess I'll see you later." I always hate this moment when you part ways with a guy that you are on unknown terms with-- do we shake hands, hug, kiss? It's so awkward and I take a step back. I just want to leave.

"See 'ya, freckles," he says with a half smile. Then, he shoves his hands into his front jean pockets, turns and starts down the sidewalk.

My heart hitches at the nickname and I watch his tall figure move away. Just when I think he's not going to turn back, he glances over a shoulder. When he catches me still standing there, watching him, he turns all the way around and keeps walking backwards. A smile curves his mouth and he lifts his hand, making it look like a phone and mouths the words "call me." Then, he winks, turns and ambles around the corner.

*Dammit.* I really like Bastian, but everything in me is screaming out a warning to stay away. He was being weird at first today and I'm not sure what was going on in his head. He seemed...off. I can't believe he invited me over for more champagne. Why didn't he just say what he meant? Want to fuck tonight? His true intention was pretty clear.

But, then he warmed up and confided about his tattoos. It must be hard not having either of your parents and losing your sister. It's hard enough not having my Mom anymore, but at least I still have both of my overprotective brothers, thank God, and even though he's completely useless, my Dad. I'm glad Bastian has Jax because his big brother is strong, smart and supportive.

I didn't know Jax before Easton, but apparently, he was a train-wreck waiting to happen. I'm glad she helped him get his life back together. Because Jax is in an amazing place now and I can tell he wants to help Bastian in every way he can.

Bastian just needs to let him.

But, I know his type too well. They don't want help. They think they have everything under control and they're infallible.

That is, until they fall. And they always do.

I watched my Dad fall and now he's sitting in a prison cell for the next 10-15 years. He must be going crazy. Like Bastian, my Dad isn't one to stick around in one place for too long. He likes to drift from one adventure to the next. A soldier of fortune who broke my poor Mother's heart.

The issue is I've never been interested in anyone like this before. It's kind of unnerving. I need some advice and decide to call Lexi. Before she met Griff, she and I were so similar. We both worked too much, avoided relationships like the plague and had to force each other to go out and be social.

But, that all changed the moment she met Griffin Lawson.

I sit down on the sidewalk, lean back against the building near the front entrance to Platinum Security and dial my friend. I know she's probably working-- she's a librarian at the Pasadena Library-- but, I'm hoping she's still on lunch.

After a few rings, she picks up. "Hey, Harlow!"

"Hey, how are you?"

"Good. What's up?"

I let out a small sigh and pull my knees up to my chest. "Got a minute?" I ask.

"Sure. I can take a break." She must notice that I sound weird. Unsure and confused. "What's wrong?"

"Well, things have been interesting here at the office."

"What do you mean?"

"I guess it kind of started when Jax's younger brother was thrown into the front door and stabbed."

"*What?*"

"Yeah, last night. After Easton's, I came back to the office to get some things done and I heard a commotion outside. When I went to check it out, I found him out on the sidewalk. I pulled the camera footage and three guys jumped him."

"Holy shit. Is he okay? Does Jax know?"

"Yeah, he's fine and Jax stopped by. Bastian is staying at Jax's apartment and I drove him there last night."

Lexi waits for me to continue, and I can almost hear her smile. "And..."

"And, um, we kind of kissed."

Lexi squeals so loudly that I have to pull the phone away from my ear.

"Lex, this isn't good."

"Of course, it is," she says in a happy voice. "Jax's little brother? Oh, my gosh, this is so exciting! I'm sooo excited for you!"

"Okay, please stop gushing because I don't know if you've heard, but Bastian is bad news."

"Oh, whatever. They're all bad news, but when the right woman comes along, these men shape up."

Maybe she's right. But, could I be the right woman for Bastian Wilder? I'm not sure she even exists, to be honest. "I guess it's why I'm calling." I drop my forehead against my knees and sigh. "Oh, God, Lex, I'm so confused. Everything in me is warning me to stay away from him. But, I swear to God, I've never been this attracted to a man. He's like fucking catnip and I just want to roll all over him."

Lexi laughs. "So roll over him."

"He's just going to hurt me. I know his type. Fuck 'em and leave 'em."

"You know, you could be talking about Griff. When we first met, he was the biggest player. Cocky and so sure of himself. I remember thinking that he was a heartbreak waiting to happen. But, I couldn't stay away from him and holed up in that hotel room with him when we were in New York...*God.* So, I know exactly how you feel. Love is a risk and it's scary, but if you can make it work, it's the best thing in the world. It's like magic."

Talk about a woman in love. Lord Almighty, I could practically see little red hearts spilling out of my phone. *Is Bastian worth the risk?* I wonder.

"My advice? Take a chance, Harlow."

I lift my head and spot Griff walking out the front door. When he sees me, he saunters over. "I have to go. Your fiancé just came out."

"Tell him I love him," she says.

"That Lexi?" he asks. When I nod, that goofy smile people get when they're madly in love appears. He motions for my phone and I hand it up to him. "Hey, Red," he says in a low voice. Everything in his tone changes the moment he talks to her and I feel a wave of jealousy.

What would it be like to have someone love me this much? I really have no idea.

After a quick, whispered conversation, Griff turns back around and hands me the phone. Just a few words with Lexi and he looks like he's walking on clouds. "Thanks," he says.

"Lexi?"

"I'm here," she says, voice sounding as dreamy as Griff's.

I roll my eyes. "I should go. I'll call you later."

"Okay. And, we're still meeting Avery for drinks this weekend. Don't forget."

"I won't. I have a feeling I'm going to need her advice, too." We say goodbye and I hang up.

Griff drops down in front of the door and examines the broken glass. I walk over and he looks up, the sun making his eyes glow like blue topaz. But, all I can think about is another pair of eyes that glow sage green with flecks of gold.

"I'm gonna run out and get a new pane of glass so we can fix this."

"Way to make yourself useful," I say.

"You know it." He stands up, dusts his jeans off. "Ryker went out to grab some lunch and I should be back in half an hour or so."

"Don't rush on my account. I can hold the fort down."

"Thanks, ShadowWalker. See you in a bit."

I open the door and head back down to my office. The rest of the day passes in a blur. Griff and Ryker fix the front door and stay busy with clients while I do my thing and find out whatever they need found.

I haven't looked at the clock since maybe two and suddenly it's dark out. Griff and Ryker stop outside my doorway. "We're heading out," Griff says. "It's almost seven o'clock, go home."

"You spend too much time here," Ryker says. "Gonna need to get you a cot."

"I just have to finish up this one thing."

They exchange a look. "Alright, well have a good night."

"You, too," I say, eyes still on my screen, and throw up a little wave.

I work another half an hour and just as I'm contemplating whether or not to brew a new pot of coffee, my email dings. I glance over at the left monitor where my email sits on the screen and do a double take.

It's from my Dad.

I hesitate then reluctantly open the new message. I've never responded to any of his emails and I don't see that changing. But, I still read them.

Curiosity killed the cat, right?

Well, his message doesn't kill me, but it hurts. A lot.

I read it twice, drag my glasses off and drop my face in my hands. He asks how I'm doing, how Dane and Rafe are and rambles on about a few other things before he gets to the point-- *I miss you, honey. I'd love it if you would come visit me. Despite everything, you're still my daughter and I love you.*

A string of curses flow through my head and I don't appreciate the guilt trip. He rarely visited me when he could...and, now I'm just supposed to drive out to Lancaster and pretend we have a normal father/daughter relationship?

*Not gonna happen,* I think.

I can't help it. I read through the email again. Part of it goes off on a weird tangent and I don't know what he's talking about. He asks if I've found anyone special. *But, avoid men who seem too sparkly, too loose to be true. And, definitely avoid Antwerp over Valentine's Day. Even if it's the love of a century.*

I have no idea what he's talking about. He's always been a little quirky, but that's just downright odd. The most upsetting thing is that he wants me to visit him. The whole thing throws me for a loop and the more I think about it, the more upset I get.

*Damn him.* Why can't he just leave me alone?

Now I can't focus on work.

Have I found anyone special? An image of Bastian fills my head.

*Well, with all that champagne in my fridge, I thought you might want to come over and have a drink.*

Suddenly, going over to visit Bastian and having a glass of champagne doesn't sound so bad. In fact, it sounds downright tempting. I really need someone to help me get my mind off my Dad and who better to do that than Bastian?

I pop into the bathroom and freshen up. I brush my teeth, pull my hair out of its ponytail and give it a shake. Then, I touch up my lip gloss.

Before I can change my mind, I head out to the Range Rover and drive it over to Jax's apartment. I pull over at the curb across the street and sit there. The minutes tick by and I feel my earlier courage plummet. *What am I doing here?*

Just as the thought echoes through my head, the front door opens and I see Bastian. He heads down the walkway, once again wearing his leather jacket over a black t-shirt with jeans. I wonder where he's going this late?

Bastian heads over to a motorcycle parked at the curb. He slides a long leg over it, sits and pulls a helmet over his head. After a few kick starts, the engine comes to life and he flips the headlights on and starts down the street.

And, I decide to follow him.

Heart in my throat, I keep my distance, headlights off, trailing him. I figure he's going to some chick's house to hook up or he's up to no good. Either way, I want to know. Maybe some dirt on him will help cool my jets and drill into me that he's bad news and convince me to stay away.

Bastian takes N. Normandie Avenue down to Koreatown and stops outside a dark, abandoned-looking building. There's nowhere for me to park, but he pulls right up between two cars and slides off the bike. I slow down, watch him disappear into a side entrance and then drive around the block, searching for a parking spot.

Finally, I found one. I'm beyond curious now and hurry back around and over to the side door of the dark building where he slipped inside. I'm surprised to see a big bouncer-looking dude guarding the door and pause. *What is going on?*

"Twenty bucks," he says.

I glance over his beefy shoulder and realize the place is packed. People are cheering and cussing and all bunched up together, attention on something. I dig a twenty dollar bill out of my purse and hand it over. When he steps aside, I make my way into the musty-smelling room. It's pretty big, but the crowd makes it feel smaller.

I have no idea how I'm going to find Bastian, but I push through the throng, trying to get a look at what the hell has everyone so absorbed. Finally, I see a makeshift area squared off by bales of hay and inside two men look like they're beating each other to death.

It's an underground fight club.

*God, it's vicious.* Flesh slams against flesh. Bare fists pound into faces and I wince when I see the one man's head snap to the side and blood flies through the air. When it splatters the people in the front row, pressed up to the hay bales, they cheer even louder.

The fight is beyond brutal and I don't understand the appeal of watching two grown men beat each other senseless. They go at it for a few rounds and then a winner is declared. My gaze wanders over the crowd, but I don't see Bastian's tall frame. Just when I decide to start wandering, I hear the announcer introduce two new fighters.

*Idiots,* I think. They're going to beat each other to a pulp and for what? Probably a measly amount of prize money. How is this entertainment? I shake my head, trying to decide if I should just leave, when I glance at the new contenders.

One of them is Bastian.

*Oh, my God.* I shove my way closer to the front, eyes glued to him. He doesn't wear a shirt and I can see the patch of gauze taped over his knife wound. *Is he crazy?* How is he going to fight when he's still injured?

The announcer jumps out of the way and suddenly Bastian and the other guy begin to circle each other, fists up. Bastian's opponent is maybe 5'9" with thick, corded muscles and a bald head. He looks dangerous and worry floods me.

Finally, my knees hit the hay bale and I can't get any closer. The meaty opponent throws a punch and Bastian easily side-steps it and slams a quick fist into the guy's side. God, Bastian is fast. He moves with a grace and speed that the other guy doesn't possess. He may be thick and strong-looking, but he is slow and lumbers while Bastian dances circles around him.

But, all it would take is one solid fist to Bastian's wound and he'd go down.

*Shit.* I lean over the bale, eyes glued to the fight. *Please, be careful,* I think. Each second of the fight seems to last an eternity and after some hits, the first round ends. I realize I'm holding my hands against my mouth, nerves strung taut, barely able to breathe.

When round two begins, his opponent wastes no time. He lunges forward, fists flying and Bastian ducks then drives up with a fist to the guy's kidney. His opponent doubles over and I realize I'm cheering and yelling right along with the rest of the crowd.

When the guy stands back up, he rears up swinging and catches Bastian's cheek with a hard hit. I gasp, cover my mouth and feel my heart stop. But, Bastian shakes it off and circles around, fists in front of his face for protection.

*Oh, my God, I'm going to have a heart attack.* Round two seems to last forever and they each get several more brutal hits in before it's over. Blood drips down Bastian's face from a cut near his eyebrow and he swipes it away with the back of his hand.

*One more round,* I tell myself. Then, it's over. *Hang in there, Bastian.*

The announcer hits a bell and Bastian and his opponent both go in for the kill. Bastian manages to get a punch into the guy's gut, but then his opponent drops and slams a meaty fist into the bandage on Bastian's side.

*Oh, my God.* Blood blossoms over the white gauze and Bastian stumbles from the pain.

"Bastian!" I scream.

At the sound of his name, he glances up, brown hair hanging in his eyes. And, that's when his opponent attacks. A fist smashes into Bastian's jaw and his head jerks to the side. But, suddenly, Bastian digs deep and spins back around, fists moving hard and with ungodly speed and precision.

I scream my bloody head off, cheering him on and ten seconds later, the beefy opponent drops. The announcer yanks Bastian's arm into the air, declaring him the winner, and that's when Bastian's gaze meets mine.

Breathing hard, blood dripping down his face, he stalks toward me and I'd take a step back, but I can't. I'm packed in like a sardine. When he reaches me, his eyes flash green and gold. "What the hell are you doing here?" he asks.

"I-I followed you," I admit.

"Fuck, Harlow." He glances over his shoulder, sees two new opponents enter the ring and swings himself over the hay bale. He drops down, his hot, sweaty, very tattooed chest pressing into me, and I look up into his handsome, bloody face. "You shouldn't be here," he says. Then, he grabs my hand and pulls me through the crowd.

"You're bleeding-"

"I'm fine."

Once we break out of the throng around the ring, he heads over to a counter where a pretty girl hands him his t-shirt and leather jacket. "Thanks, Britt," he says and she bats long lashes at him.

"Any time, Bastian. Good fight," she adds then looks me over, her smile fading. "Mickey has your money."

"Thanks," he says and pulls me along. "What're you doing here?" he hisses.

"I already told you-"

"Yeah, I heard, you followed me. But, why?"

*Oh, great, now I sound like a complete stalker.* "Actually, I drove over to your place. To see if that offer for a drink was still open?"

He abruptly stops walking and I slam into his shoulder. Hot hazel eyes slant down and meet mine. "It's still open," he says in a husky voice and my stomach somersaults.

My eyes dip to his lips and, God, I want to kiss him again. Despite the blood there.

"Let me just get my money," he says.

We make our way over to an overweight man who wears a fedora and lots of jewelry. "Good job tonight, Bastian." He counts off a wad of cash and hands it over.

"Thanks, Mickey," Bastian says and tucks it into a pocket.

"Who's the pretty lady?" he asks and winks at me.

"Harlow," I say.

"Hang onto this one," Mickey tells Bastian. "Saw her cheering louder than anyone," he adds and I feel my cheeks redden.

Bastian nods his head and guides me out a back door. Then, he stops, slides his jacket on and pulls a pack of cigarettes out. As he lights one up, he fixes an intent gaze on me. He inhales then breathes the smoke out through his nose, reminding me of a dragon. "You cheered for me?" he asks.

"Yeah. I mean, I wasn't going to cheer for that Vin Diesel guy over you."

A smile curves his mouth. "Well, that was nice of you, freckles."

I watch him smoke, unable to look away from the way his lips hold the cigarette. Kind of loose and languid. Then, he pulls it out and touches a finger to his tongue to flick away a piece of tobacco. "Sorry, if the smoke bothers you," he says and exhales to the side. "But, I have to unwind."

"It doesn't," I say. "My Dad smokes."

"It's a disgusting habit, right? Settles my nerves, though."

I reach down, pluck the cigarette from his hand and inhale. As I release the smoke, I say, "I used to sneak a few with my brothers when we were younger."

His mouth opens, closes and then he swallows hard. When I hand him the cigarette back, our fingers touch and it's electric. Like a current passes between us. My heart speeds up and he wraps his lips around it for another puff. "You're not like anyone I've ever met," he says in a low voice.

"Is that a good thing?" I ask.

"It's a very good thing," he confirms and finishes the cigarette. He stubs it out against the side of a steel trash can and tosses it away. "Now...about that drink..."

"Meet you back at your place?"

Something flashes in his eyes and he nods. "See you soon."

On the drive back to Jax's apartment, my mind whirls. I give him credit, he definitely got my mind off my Dad. I'm still trying to wrap my head around seeing him in that ring tonight, fighting. I didn't like it and, at the same time, there was something incredibly hot seeing him shirtless and so raw.

I want him. Why deny it?

When we get back to Jax's, I park the car and see Bastian already sliding off the bike. I get out, lock the car and cross the street.

"Thought you might ditch me," he says, mouth edging up.

"Why would you think that?"

"I don't know. Last I heard, you were all champagned-out."

"Guess I changed my mind."

"Guess so." He eyes me then nods his head toward the door. "C'mon."

We go into the dark apartment and he flips a light switch, sliding out of the leather jacket. When the bright light illuminates his body, I suck in a sharp breath. Bruises, swelling and dried blood cover him. "Your side," I say and scrunch my face up at the blood-soaked bandage.

Bastian glances down and then peels it off with a grunt. The entire wound re-opened and it didn't look good.

"Kitchen," I say and head over to the counter where I spot the medical kit from the office. I open it up and pull out a packet of wipes. "Sit," I order him.

Bastian arches a brow and hops up on the counter. "Bossy, bossy," he comments.

"You haven't seen bossy yet," I tell him with a smile. I find a clean towel and run it under warm water. Then I turn, move between his legs and take a deep breath before lifting it and running it over his chest. His chest hitches, almost like he's holding his breath, and I run the cloth over each scratch and cut and then wipe the dried blood away around the knife wound.

Damn, he has a nice body. All lean and tight. Very athletic. *Like a swimmer,* I think. Even though there's no blood there, I drag the towel over his washboard abs. When I look up, I see his eyes slide shut, nostrils flare.

When they open again, I try not to notice the raw desire I see. Instead, I focus on cleaning the wound with alcohol. He hisses in a breath and squirms.

"It'll be a miracle if this doesn't get infected," I say. "What were you thinking? Fighting when you were still hurt?"

"I don't always think things through. I just knew I needed some cash and fighting is an easy way to get it."

I rinse out the towel and move back between his legs, now focusing on running it over his face. He grabs my wrist and pins me with a hot look. Heat pools low in my belly.

"I'm going to take a shower," he murmurs. His words linger in the air, like an invitation he's waiting for me to accept. But, I don't say anything and his long fingers finally release my wrist. A muscle flexes in his cheek.

"Okay," I say and spin away, rinsing the towel in the sink, trying to act nonchalant. "When you get out, we need to put a bandage on your side."

He slips off the counter and stands there for a moment. As though he's waiting for something. Then, he gives a sharp nod and walks away. And, I sink against the counter, my heart beating so hard it feels like it's going to rip from my chest.

It takes Bastian all of five minutes to shower and when he reappears, shirtless and in loose pajama bottoms, I can't help when my gaze dips and catches sight of that "X" tattoo below his navel. It's late and I know I should leave. But, instead, I walk over with fresh gauze and tape.

"Looks a little better," I say.

"Feels better, too," he says. "I took an ibuprofen. Actually, I took three."

I just shake my head, place the gauze over the wound and rip a piece of tape with my teeth. Once the bandage is secure, I step back. "There. All set."

I can't pull my eyes away from the "X" and his low-slung pajama bottoms.

"Thank you," he says. "Still interested in that glass of champagne? We can celebrate my win."

I should say no, walk out now. But, that's not what I want. Not even close.

"Sure," I say and follow him back into the kitchen. I put the medical tape back in the kit and watch him open another bottle of Easton's favorite champagne. He pops the cork, pours two glasses and hands me one.

"Thanks for coming to my rescue. Again," he adds and clinks the edge of his glass against mine.

"No problem," I say with a small smile. I take a sip, watching him over the rim just like he's watching me. God, it's like this invisible current passes between us and my pulse begins to pound when he reaches over, takes my glass and sets them both on the counter.

Then, he turns back and something begins to flow within me--

low, hot and thick like lava-- and when I lift my eyes to meet his, our gazes lock and hold.

"Why did you come here tonight?" he asks in a husky voice.

*Isn't it obvious?*

Instead of responding with words, I take a step closer and hook my fingers in his pajama bottoms. He tenses at first, but then his green eyes flare and he slams his mouth down against mine. I moan and lift my arms, raking my fingers through his thick hair. Yes, Bastian definitely knows how to take my mind off everything because when he's kissing me like this, everything else disappears except the two of us.

Sensations fill me. Desire, need and want roar through my body and it's been so long since I've allowed myself to just let go with a man. Completely let go. My bed has been empty for far too long and loneliness makes me wanton.

Makes me throw caution to the wind and I push into Bastian, crushing my breasts against his chest and sliding my tongue against his. I'm done feeling alone, done worrying about what may or may not happen if I sleep with this man. He's the only man who has managed to snag my attention and make my blood boil so why fight it?

It's time to stop overthinking and just feel.

When we finally come up for air, we're both breathing heavily and clarity strikes. I want Bastian Wilder like I've never wanted another man. And, I'm going to have him.

I reach down and lift my shirt up and over my head. I toss it on a chair and unbutton my jeans. When I'm finally brave enough to look up, I'm scared he's going to be looking at me with disgust or rejection or disappointment.

*No, definitely not.* His gaze drops, eyeing my black satin bra, and his nostrils flare. I slide the zipper down on my jeans and he watches, hazel eyes hooded, completely enthralled. I shimmy out of them and stand before him in my skimpy, black satin underthings.

"You're so fucking beautiful," he whispers. He moves closer, like a panther stalking its prey. I swallow hard and when he reaches me, he glides his fingers up my arms and goosebumps break out over my skin.

His fingers skim over the tops of my shoulders, across my collarbone and then up to cup my face in his hands. When he leans down to kiss me again, it's not what I expect at all. It's slow and sensual and the way he holds my face is beyond gentle.

I tilt my head back, deepening the kiss, and a few languid moments later he pulls his mouth away, dragging it down, leaving a trail of wet kisses along my neck. Downward still...I feel his tongue trace along the swell of my breast and I push closer, giving him full access. He reaches around, unsnaps the bra and the straps slide down my arms.

His mouth dips down again and he pulls a nipple into his mouth. Tugging, sucking, swirling. *Oh, my God.* It's like an electrical charge zaps through me and I gasp. The connection is white-hot and I dig my nails into his upper arms. His muscles flex and it's like digging my fingernails into granite.

I don't even realize I'm making this humming noise in the back of my throat until he comments. "You sound like a hummingbird."

I pull back, breathing hard, trying to catch my breath, but fuck it. It's impossible with him looking at me like that. Like he's going to devour me whole. "Sorry."

"Don't be sorry. I like it."

I feel my cheeks heat up and I run my hands over his chest, eyeing the ink. My gaze zooms in on the barbell piercings and I lean forward and grab one in my mouth, wrapping my lips around it. My tongue circles it and my teeth tug.

"Jesus," he hisses, sliding his hands through my hair, back arching.

"Did it hurt?" I ask, nipping all around the piercing.

"A little pain is good. Makes the pleasure all that much better."

I wonder if his words are a foreshadow of tonight. I've never been into kinky sex, but Bastian isn't like anyone I've ever been with and I get the feeling he likes to push limits and boundaries. My nerves kick in and I pull back. "Am I going to need a safe word?" I ask.

He bursts out laughing and shakes his head. "Oh, freckles."

Next thing I know, he scoops me up into his arms and carries me down to the small extra bedroom at the end of the hall. "Don't tell anyone, but I have a traditional side, too," he whispers.

My heart thunders as he lays me down on the bed, pushing me back and covering me with his large body. He dips his head, begins kissing my neck and my eyes flutter shut. Good God, he smells amazing. Potent masculinity.

"Why do you smell like strawberries?" he asks, nibbling on my neck.

My eyes pop open. "You don't like strawberries?"

Bastian pulls back and looks down at me. "I fucking love strawberries."

"Oh, good." I smile. "Must be my shampoo."

He buries his face in my hair and inhales. "Mm, yeah," he murmurs.

My stomach drops when I feel him hook his fingers in my panties and begin to slide them down. God, I'm nervous. I haven't done this in a long time and Bastian is so edgy, such a bad boy. I don't know what he expects, but I don't want to disappoint him.

He must feel me tense up because after he tosses the satin panties, he moves back up, his gaze searching mine. "What's wrong?" he asks.

"I'm just...nervous." And, naked. Like completely naked under this incredibly hot man covered in ink and who is probably into all sorts of things like BDSM and sex toys that I have no idea about.

God, his hazel eyes are so intense it feels like he's looking into my soul. "Why?" he asks and trails a long finger along my jaw.

"You're just really..." I swallow hard. "Intense."

"And that scares you?"

"No, I like it. I'm just scared..." I bite my lip. "I'm just scared I'm going to be too vanilla for you."

Something flashes in those hazel eyes. Something hot and fierce. "Freckles, you are the furthest thing from vanilla," he says and captures my mouth in a long, sizzling kiss. He moves between my legs and the soft cotton of his pajama bottoms presses against my wet center. When I feel the hard ridge behind the thin fabric, I scrape my nails down his back and push up.

"Vanilla," he scoffs. "You're so fucking spicy." He drags his mouth down, sliding his tongue along the curve of my breast, down around my navel. "So hot..." he murmurs, moving down my thigh, then around to the inside, "...you burn...my...mouth..."

When his mouth makes contact with the hot center between my legs, my hips jerk up and I bite back a cry. I twist the sheet in one hand and grab his hair in my other. As he spreads my folds and licks, laps and sucks, I feel feverish. The pleasure consumes me and I twist and moan, but he grabs my hips, slides his hands under my ass and lifts me up for better access. "I want you to come on my tongue," he says.

*Oh, Lord. At this rate, it won't be long,* I think.

I'm at his mercy and his tongue is doing such wicked things that I drop my head back and moan. "Bastian, *God,*" I cry as the first wave of an orgasm hits me. My entire body trembles under his skilled mouth and pleasure consumes me. Again and again.

Breathing hard, satiated like never before, I reach down with my other hand, twine it through the longer, damp hair on top of his head and yank him back up.

"Ow," he says with a chuckle and rubs his scalp.

"Sorry," I say. "You've got me all worked up."

"You needed me back up here for something?" he teases.

I glance down at his pajama bottoms. "It kind of feels weird being the only one without clothes on," I admit.

"I kind of like it," he whispers and runs his fingers down my side in a feather-soft caress. I feel the cool metal of his rings and tingles race up and down my entire body.

Feeling emboldened, I reach down and cup him. His body tenses and he lets out a breathy sigh. God, there's a lot in his pajama bottoms, I think, my heart pounding.

Bastian jerks back, shoves his bottoms down, kicking them to the floor. I get a glimpse of...well, quite a bit and Sebastian Wilder is not lacking in any way, shape or form. He reaches for a foil packet, rips it open and I watch him roll the condom on as heat liquifies low in my belly and then finds its way between my legs.

When he moves back between my thighs, I part them further, wrap them around his waist and pull him closer. His thick, hot length hovers at my entrance, pressing lightly, and I flick my gaze up to meet his which glows an unholy green. "Do it," I tell him. "Fuck me. *Hard.*"

Heat radiates off him and he needs no further invitation. Bastian rears up with a grunt, shoving into me hard and fast. I cry out, feeling the pleasure-pain as my body stretches, trying to accommodate him. He pauses, gaze searing into mine, making sure I'm okay. "Don't stop," I hiss.

He begins to move, thrusting into me with long, powerful strokes that seem to hit all of my sensitive areas just right. So right that I'm panting and once again caught up in rippling waves that make me feel like I'm going to burst into a thousand beams of light.

I'm on the edge when he reaches a hand down between our bodies and starts massaging me where I'm already so hot and swollen. My lower body instantly tightens around him and everything inside me explodes. It's too much, I literally can't bear it, and a scream rips from my throat.

Bastian isn't far behind me and I feel his movements get jerky. Suddenly, his entire body goes rigid and shudders. With a long groan, he finds his release and then drops beside me.

*Holy shit,* I think.

# 10

# BASTIAN

"Holy shit," I rasp. I can't remember the last time I had an orgasm that intense. It takes a minute to catch my breath and I look over at Harlow and realize she's caught up in the same unbelievable afterglow.

When I finally get it together, I slip out of bed and pad off to the bathroom. After I take care of the condom, I catch a glimpse of my reflection in the mirror. I look out of it, still passion-dazed, and I feel like I was just knocked out in a fight. TKO.

Vanilla. *Is she insane?* Well, that little vanilla wafer just rocked my fucking world. No doubt about it.

*God, seriously, what just happened?* I'm usually much more vocal during sex. More playful. And, I last a helluva lot longer.

But, she said I was intense so I held back a little because I didn't want to scare her.

*Am I going to need a safe word?*

She's really too much and I couldn't help but laugh at her wide blue-gray eyes and serious tone. I don't know if she had visions of leather, paddles and handcuffs or what, but the last thing I wanted was for Harlow to run.

I wanted to tell her she's safe with me. That I'd never hurt her.

But, that would be a lie.

At least I can say I made her feel good. There's no doubt that she enjoyed our little encounter as much as I did.

Feeling a surge of masculine pride, I step out of the bathroom and hear her moving around in the living room. I wander over to see her on the edge of the couch, fully dressed, and slipping her shoes back on. *Wait a minute.*

Harlow looks up, face still flushed from multiple orgasms. "I should go," she says and stands up, searching for her purse.

My mouth drops open in surprise, but I quickly close it. I mean, if she wants to go, I'm not going to stop her. I just kind of thought she'd spend the night. *I'm such an idiot.*

I guess she got what she came for and now she's out. After that mind-blowing romp, I thought-- *hoped*-- she'd stay the night. I haven't even begun to get started with Harlow Vaughn yet.

But, I'm not going to pretend it doesn't piss me off. And, hurt my feelings a little.

"Why are you running?" I ask.

She spins around. "What?"

"You heard me. And this is the second time you've done it."

She opens her mouth to deny it, but then realizes I'm right. "I don't know what you want from me."

*What do I want from her?* Hell, I don't know. All I know is she intrigues the hell out of me and, for the first time, I don't want a woman to leave after having sex with her. "Whatever you're willing to give," I answer in a quiet voice.

Emotion moves over her face then she shakes her head. "I'm sorry. I have to go."

She practically runs to the door, yanks it open and then finally looks back. "Bye," she says in a soft voice.

"Bye," I answer, getting more and more pissed. After she closes the door, I kick the couch and hurt my toe. "Fuck," I swear and drop down, still naked and feeling...

I feel used. *Slam, bam, thank you Bastian.*

*Wow.* No one has ever run out on me that fast after sex. They usually want to hang out and cuddle and I'm the one trying to dash out or move them along. Well, no doubt about it. Karma just came around and kicked me in the balls.

I don't like it. I had plans for her and for us tonight. So much for that, I think, and run a frustrated hand through my messy hair. Messy because she kept running her fingers through it and pulling it so damn hard.

I grit my teeth and curse.

What is it about Harlow that's making me a little crazy? I couldn't stop thinking about her before we slept together so now it's going to be even harder. I've never met anyone like her. Not even close. Besides being incredibly smart and beautiful, I honestly enjoy her company. She keeps me guessing. And, she doesn't treat me like a screw-up.

*Get it together, Bastian.* I have no regrets and I'm glad we just had sex. But, I need to stay focused. Nix any emotions creeping in and accept the situation for what it really is. This isn't some story with a fairytale ending and I have to remember that she's a means to an end.

Tonight's hot encounter was an added bonus. Hopefully, a way to increase her trust in me. But, after the way she bolted, that's up for debate.

*She's only a plaything until you deliver her to Angelo.*

Harlow Vaughn is the key to saving myself and I feel bad, but it's either her or me. And, let's face it. I barely know her. This should be an easy sacrifice that will get me out of a huge jam.

*Then how come it doesn't feel that way?* I wonder.

Instead, I feel like the bad guy and when all is said and done, Harlow could possibly get hurt. Angelo is vicious, I remind myself. If she doesn't cooperate…

Would he hurt her?

Shit, I honestly don't know.

And, I do know her a little better even though I don't want to admit it. I know what makes her writhe, come and scream. I know what she tastes like, smells like and how she moves beneath me.

*Strawberries and cream.*

My cock starts to get hard again. I need to cool off. I head back down to the bathroom and take a cold shower. I guess it helps. A little.

It's getting late and instead of fucking Harlow all night, I drop down in the empty bed, naked and alone. I turn my face into the pillow where her head was not even a half hour ago and breathe deeply. So sweet.

When my phone rings, I reach over, grab it off the nightstand and hope to see her name on the caller i.d. But, no. Unknown Caller.

"Yeah," I say, laying back down against the strawberry-scented pillow.

"Always so polite, aren't you?" Angelo says.

Great, I think and roll my eyes. Angelo Savini is the perfect way to end my night. "Yeah," I repeat.

He gives a low chuckle then gets straight to business. "I want you to bring Harlow Vaughn to the Velvet Room tomorrow night. Two of my guys will make contact at midnight at the first floor bar in the southwest corner adjacent to the emergency exit. Make sure she's there at the end of the bar so they can slip her out quick and easy."

My heart thumps and I suddenly feel sick to my stomach. "Sure," I manage to say.

"You get one shot to make amends, Bastian. Don't fuck it up."

Angelo disconnects the call and my eyes slide shut. *Shit.* I don't want to do this. I never thought I had much of a conscience but, suddenly, it's making itself known. It's like an angel sits on one shoulder and a devil on the other.

*You can't do this to her.*

*You don't have a choice.*

I drop the phone, scrub a hand over the light scruff on my lower face and feel my gut twist.

At this point, I don't even know how I'm going to get her to agree to go out to a club with me, anyway. After anything happens between us, she bolts. But, she always seems to come back, I think. Maybe she's having a hard time forgetting me like I am forgetting her.

I hope so. In fact, I hope she's up all night, remembering how my mouth felt on her pussy. How my cock felt buried deep inside her. I want her to be as hot and uncomfortable as I am, tossing and turning, full of heated, lusty thoughts.

I look down and see the sheet tent above my groin.

*Goddammit.*

What am I going to do? I think.

Other than jack off for the next minute, I have no fucking idea.

## 11

# HARLOW

By the time I get back to my apartment, it's after eleven and I've never been more confused in my life.

Being with Bastian blindsided me tonight. I had a feeling it was going to be good, but more in the quick, rough, get him out of my system kind of way. I had no idea he would slow down and take the time to pleasure me like that. God, that mouth of his. No one has ever made my entire body quiver and throb the way he did.

It still throbs.

Because I can still feel him inside me. Still feel the way he moved and filled me up.

A shower does nothing to cool me off and I find myself under my covers, thoughts of tattoos and piercings and Bastian's hazel eyes swirling through my head. The man is utterly delicious and, God help me, I want him again.

But, I'm sure he's done with me. Men like Bastian don't hang around and he basically told me he doesn't do relationships.

*I like to come and go whenever I want. I hate feeling tied down.*

It's not easy, but I finally fall asleep.

And, I dream of Bastian.

The next day, it's Saturday but that doesn't stop me from going into the office for a few hours. Actually, it's more like six hours. But, I don't mind because it helps keep my mind off last night. Until Bastian calls.

I look down at my ringing phone, heart in my throat. I'm not sure if I should answer, but I'm dying to know why he's calling. I take a deep breath, go against everything in my gut that tells me not to, and answer.

"Hi, Bastian," I say in a voice that comes out far huskier than I intend.

"Hey, freckles," he says in an equally low voice. A shiver runs down my spine as I wait for him to reveal why he's calling. "Got a sec?"

"Sure."

"I, ah, guess I just wanted to let you know that last night was amazing."

My stomach somersaults. "Yeah, it was."

"And, I wish it hadn't ended so fast."

*Oh, God, why is he doing this to me?* All I want to do is stay strong and keep my distance, but I can feel myself caving at his softly-spoken words. "Bastian-"

"Harlow, I'm not going to pretend I'm some kind of saint and never have one-night stands. Because I do. It's just...I never wanted to wake up next to anyone until you."

My heart constricts and I suck in a breath. He's telling me what I want to hear. Easing my fears.

And, it makes me more suspicious than ever.

I'm not exactly sure how to respond. I wish I could run him through one of my programs and see if he's lying. I can't help but question his sincerity because he reminds me so much of my Dad and he was a first-class liar.

"Harlow?"

I clear my throat. "Sorry, I'm just really wary when it comes to men and relationships."

"Because you were hurt before?"

"Something like that," I say. Yeah, I was definitely hurt, but not by a lover. By family. The very people who you were supposed to be able to trust completely.

"I'm sorry," he says. "But, I still want to spend more time with you. Can I take you out tonight?"

"Like on a date?" I ask, completely taken off-guard. I was expecting a booty call not an invitation to dinner. Not that I'm complaining. I'm just really surprised.

He chuckles. "Yeah. Is that okay?"

"I'm meeting the girls tonight for drinks at five."

"So, how about after?"

Damn, he's being persistent. "Um, sure," I say slowly.

"Where are you meeting them?"

"Some martini bar in Hollywood."

"Perfect. Why don't I pick you up after? There's a great Italian place over there we can go to. I mean, if you like Italian food?"

"Yeah, I love it."

"Great. Text me after your drinks."

*Oh, no, what am I doing?* "Okay," I say. After we hang up, my head spins. Bastian Wilder is taking me out tonight. *What the fuck?* I had him pegged as an aloof bad boy from the moment I saw him. A man who would be there for me if I wanted some quick, rough sex. Not a man who would call and ask me out on a date. Especially after saying he wanted to wake up next to me.

I'm so confused and, secretly, a little excited.

After that call, I'm not going to be getting any more work done so I decide to head home and start getting ready. Tonight, I'm putting some effort into my appearance. No ponytail and minimal makeup.

Later, in my bathroom, I spread out my measly makeup collection and get to work. I line my eyes, add a dash of sparkly shadow, mascara and a shimmery gloss. Then, I brush my dark hair until it shines. After spritzing myself with my go-to fragrance Hanae by Hanae Mori, I pause, lift my wrist up and sniff. I forgot the perfume has notes of wild strawberries and I instantly think of Bastian.

The wicked part inside me hopes it drives him crazy.

Lastly, I slip into a cute top, black leggings and boots.

We're meeting at a new martini bar and I can't believe my normally limited consumption of alcohol is now rolling into night three.

But, then again, I can't believe I had sex last night, either.

Apparently, I'm easy to read because the moment I sit down with Lexi and Avery, they exchange a look.

"You slept with him!" Lexi exclaims, brown eyes wide in delight.

Avery's mouth drops open then curves in a smile. "Spill it," she says. "We want to know everything about Jax's little brother."

I neither confirm nor deny it. And, there is nothing *little* about Jax's brother, I think. "Can I order a drink first?" I ask.

We study the menu of specialty drinks and place our orders with a server. Lexi orders a peppermint drop martini, Avery decides on a salted caramel one and I can't help but get a chocolate covered strawberry martini.

The drinks are beyond delicious and we swap them, taking tastes of each other's. Then, they focus their attention on me and wait with baited breath for all of the juicy details.

I take a fortifying drink. "So, neither of you ever met Bastian?"

"No!" Lexi says.

"Easton hasn't even met him," Avery says.

"Well, he's..." *Hmm.* How does one describe the utter yumminess that is Sebastian Wilder? "He's very edgy."

"Tattoos and a motorcycle?" Lexi asks, not in the least bit surprised.

"Definitely tattoos," I confirm. "Like everywhere. And some piercings and he wears these chunky rings." I don't even realize I lick my lips until they both dissolve into a fit of giggles.

"You are a smitten kitten," Lexi teases.

But, I shake my head. "That's the problem. Griff and Ryker told me he's trouble. They had nothing good to say about him."

"Seriously? Those two have a lot of nerve," Lexi says.

"Talk about the pot calling the kettle black," Avery adds.

"I don't recommend listening to Griff and Ryker when it comes to matters of the heart. Or, Jax," Lexi adds. "Those three alpha men think they know everything, but when it comes to love, trust me. They're still learning."

For a moment, I don't say anything, just twirl my straw. Then, I take a deep breath and burst out my biggest fear. "I really like him, you guys, but I don't know how he feels. He's definitely not one to stick around long or have anything serious. I'm scared if I don't stay away, he'll break my heart. But, God, I can't stop thinking about him."

"I think you owe it to yourself to see where this goes. I've never heard you talk about anyone like this before."

"I had a crush on Ryker for almost ten years before I was brave enough to tell him," Avery admits. "And, he had felt the same way about me all along. Being upfront and honest is better than losing time together. That's what I learned, anyway."

Maybe they were right. Both Lexi and Avery found love recently, but it wasn't easy.

"It's not always hearts and flowers in the beginning," Avery says. "Don't forget, Ryker hated me. For *years*," she adds and we all chuckle. "It took him a minute to get over himself and come around."

Ryker had blamed Avery for the death of his SEAL team, but the two recently uncovered information that proved she was framed and they faced down a string of bad guys together in Columbia. Along the way, they realized their love for one another far outweighed their past misunderstandings.

"Trust me. In the beginning, Griff was no picnic, either."

We all laugh again. No, these big, tough men at Platinum Security were far from perfect and suffocating behind their walls. They dwelled in the past and did everything they could to numb the demons that haunted them.

Easton, Lexi and Avery changed all that. They brought love, light and happiness to a few very damaged men. But, Bastian is different. He's not so much damaged, I think, but more just wild. He likes living on the edge and pushing limits. I don't think he's running from anything.

I just think he's a loner who isn't looking for anything permanent.

"You said Bastian is staying at Jax's?" Lexi asks.

As I nod, the server brings us another round. *God, these drinks are strong.* But, when I hear Lexi mention Bastian, I take a long sip. "We had lunch yesterday and then I sort of went over there last night."

They burst into smiles and little squeals.

I cover my face then peek between my fingers. "He is so...damn...good."

They laugh. "Details, please," Lexi says.

"He just knows what he's doing, you know?" Both Lexi and Avery sigh and nod in agreement. "And, he's so ridiculously hot. The combination is going to be my undoing."

I look down and realize I'm shredding my napkin into a million little pieces.

"So, what are you going to do?" Avery asks, blue eyes full of concern.

I shrug. "I don't know. I ran out of there so fast last night, I think his head spun."

"Bet he wasn't used to that," Lexi says.

"God, I wish I could just hack into his heart and program him to fall in love with me," I say.

"Unfortunately for you, he's not a computer."

"Look, we don't know much about Bastian, but from my experience with Ryker, my advice is follow your heart. That's what we did and I've never been happier."

Lexi nods, brown eyes shining. "She's right, Harlow. Until Griff, I never knew love like this existed."

Maybe they're right, I think. Maybe I should just jump and see what happens. Hopefully, he will be there to catch me. If not, I'll hit the ground and shatter. It's a scary risk.

But, isn't that love? Scary and unpredictable?

Lexi and Avery both took a chance, jumped and their men caught them.

If I'm brave enough to leap, I wonder if Bastian will catch me?

"Well," I say and glance down at the time on my phone, "I kind of left one detail out." Their eyebrows raise in unison and I can't help but smile. "He called me this afternoon and invited me to dinner. I'm supposed to let him know when we're done here and he's picking me up."

Lexi claps her hands and Avery just smirks and finishes up her drink. "Don't let us keep you," Avery says.

Five minutes later, we head out and I know my friends aren't going anywhere until they get a glimpse of Bastian. When he rolls up to the curb in the P.S. Range Rover, I spot him instantly and my heart rate increases by what feels like a thousand beats a minute.

Bastian slides out and saunters over, all lanky confidence and charm. He wears a sage green Henley which matches his eyes and a pair of jeans. His brown hair is mussed and sexy, a light scruff covers his jaw and he wears his usual chunky rings and beaded and leather bracelets.

His gaze slides to Avery and Lexi before he steps up and gives me a hug. "Hey, freckles," he says, breath warm at my ear. His arms feel so good wrapped around me and the moment he steps back, I look over at my smirking friends.

"Bastian, this is Lexi and this is Avery," I say.

They each shake his big hand and exchange glances.

"Nice to meet you," he says and slides an arm around my waist.

"You, too. We've all been dying to meet Jax's mysterious brother," Lexi says.

His mouth edges up. "Here I am. Hope your expectations weren't too high."

"If you're hanging out with Harlow, our expectations are extremely high," Avery says with a smile. And, even though her tone is teasing, she's warning him to be on his best behavior or there will be hell to pay. God, I love my friends.

"We don't want to keep you," Lexi says and gives me a hug. Avery hugs me goodbye next and then they tell Bastian it was nice meeting him and turn away with little waves. "Have fun!"

I wave goodbye and turn to Bastian. "They insisted on meeting you," I say with a smile.

"Lexi is engaged to Griff?"

"Yes. And, Avery just married Ryker. The guys at the office are dropping like flies," I joke.

"Sounds like it. Maybe they know something I don't," he adds in a low voice. "C'mon."

As his long fingers wrap around mine and he walks me to the Range Rover, I hope to God that I'm not about to make a huge mistake.

And, if I leap or inevitably fall, I pray that Bastian will catch me.

## 12

# BASTIAN

Forty-five minutes later, Harlow and I sit across from each other at a small corner table. It's intimate, private and she looks stunning in the candle glow. So much so that I can't tear my gaze away.

The server just set plates of manicotti in front of us and I reach for my glass of red wine, completely absorbed in the way she finishes telling a story about her older brother Dane.

I had no idea she has two brothers who are former military. I'm not going to deny that it makes me a little nervous. If they're anything like Ryker, they're probably going to be 6'5", built like granite and know 10 different ways to kill a man in less than 10 seconds.

I get the feeling that if they find out I hurt their little sister, I'm going to meet them and it won't be under good circumstances.

*Shit.*

"So, Dane is in San Diego?"

She shakes her head and cuts into the steaming manicotti. "Not anymore. Now, he's up north in Coalinga where he's in charge of the SEAL sniper course."

*Fucking great.* Her older brother is a sniper. Go figure.

My throat goes dry and I take another sip of wine.

"They both move around a lot so I don't get to see them as much as I'd like," she says.

"What about your parents?" I ask, loving the way the soft candlelight makes her skin glow. I'm not sure what is different tonight, but she looks even better than usual. Her thick dark hair is sleek and straight and my fingers itch to run through it.

"My Mom died and my Dad..." Her gaze drops and she fidgets with her wine glass. "We're not close."

I nod. "Sorry to hear that. I lost my parents when I was ten. We were all really close so it was hard."

"Where did you, Jax and Madison go after they died?" she asks.

A smile curves my mouth when I think of good 'ol Auntie Rita. "My Aunt Rita. Bless her heart for taking on the three of us," I say and chuckle. "She tried to keep us on the straight and narrow path, but Jax and I were hellions. We skipped Sunday school, fell asleep during church and tortured Maddy endlessly."

"Poor Aunt Rita," she commiserates and the smile she sends my way makes my heart constrict.

I'm not sure what gets me talking, but memories flood my head. "A part of me really misses that. The old days when life was more simple and if youth led you astray, there was always someone to pull you back. Guide you back to the light and away from the dark. That was my Aunt Rita."

"She sounds like she was a really good person. Not many people would take three young kids in like that."

I finally take a bite of my dinner and feel this overwhelming and completely foreign need to share my childhood with the woman who sits across from me. I have no idea why, but once I start going there's no shutting me up. "She was the best. Died a few years ago, but when she was alive, she knew how to live life to the fullest. She had this group of older women who used to come to the house every week and play cards. Man, could they gamble."

We both laugh.

"And, they drank like fish. Jax and I used to sneak into the kitchen once their card game got going and sneak hits of gin or vodka. Auntie

Rita used to make this slush-- it was vodka, pineapple juice and 7-Up, I think. That shit was strong and knocked us on our ass a few times."

"Bad boys," she says, a twinkle in those steel-blue eyes.

"Always," I admit. My thoughts turn to my brother and I frown.

"What?" she asks.

It's interesting how quickly she can read me. A little unnerving, too. "I was just thinking I can't believe that Jax is married. And, to a movie star. Leave it to him," I say, trying to keep my voice light.

But, Harlow must hear the uncertainty. "I know you haven't met yet, but Easton is a really sweet person. You're going to love her."

"I don't know. I guess it's just weird. I've never had to share Jax with anyone. Even though I haven't been around lately, we're still close. But, now that he has her..."

"You're his brother. He's always going to need you in his life," she says. "In fact, I get the feeling he'd like it if you came around more often. Maybe even stayed in LA."

Other than Jax, I never had any reason to stay here. But, now as I look at Harlow, I wonder if maybe she could be that reason. *Dammit.* I give my head a shake and force myself to remember why I even invited her out tonight.

So I can hand her over to Angelo.

Speaking of which, I need to make sure she wants to continue this and go to the club with me.

*And, what exactly is this?* I wonder. A date? A farce?

A dark lie, I realize.

But, I don't want to think about that now and instead, I ask Harlow more about working at Platinum Security. It sounds like she loves it and she tells me that their little dysfunctional family has come to mean a lot to her. I feel a twinge of jealousy. It sounds like something that I'd like to have in my life, too.

Problem is, I never put down roots.

"So, tell me what it's like being a hacker."

"Computer specialist," she corrects me.

"Oh, my mistake," I say with a teasing smile.

"I love it. There's nothing quite like it-- having the power to be whoever you want and to break into anything, anywhere in the world, without ever leaving your office. To literally have every answer at your fingertips."

*Huh*. I never thought about it that way. "So, in a way, it's freeing?"

She considers my words then nods. "Yeah, you could say that."

"How did you meet Jax?"

"Through Griff. He referred me to your brother once the company got going. I know they had a rough time in the beginning, but then it took off after Easton hired Jax."

"To protect her from a stalker, right?"

"Right. And, the rest is history."

"I'm still trying to wrap my head around the fact that he married a famous movie star. Shit, two of her movies were on TV last night and I thought, hey, there's my new sister-in-law." I smile and Harlow takes a sip of wine, eyes sparkling in the candlelight.

"It is a little weird at first, but you get used to it. I don't even think of Easton as famous anymore. Did you see her movie poster hanging in Jax's office?"

I nod.

"Griff and Ryker hung it up as a joke before they were officially together. I don't think he thought it was quite as funny as they did."

I chuckle and take another bite of manicotti. "Jax can get a little touchy when he's not in a good mood. Trust me, I grew up with him."

When the waiter brings us another bottle of red wine, we exchange a surprised look. "Um, we didn't order this," I say.

"Courtesy of Lexi and Avery," he says and uncorks the bottle. "They hope you're having a lovely evening."

"Oh, my God," Harlow says and bursts out laughing. "Those two!"

I love her low, breathy laugh. It tangles me up inside. Makes me smile. God, this woman mystifies me and I can't seem to get enough of her. We end up sitting in that dim corner for two more hours, finishing the complimentary bottle of red wine, sharing a dessert and endless, lingering looks.

It's getting late, I realize, but goddammit, I don't want to leave. I could sit here and keep talking. But, I have to get Harlow to the club.

After I sign the bill, I suddenly feel like everything I just ate and drink is going to come up and splatter all over the table.

I take a deep breath and swallow down a sip of water. Even though I'm completely sober, I can tell Harlow is buzzing from two martinis and two bottles of wine. *That should just make it easier, right?* She won't even realize what's happening until I'm gone.

"So, there's this pretty cool place nearby. The Velvet Room?" I say.

"Ooh, let's go!" she says.

Yeah, she may be a little more than tipsy. *Shit. I'm such a fucking asshole.*

"I haven't been out to a club in years," she announces, eyes bright.

I force a smile and we both stand up. I feel sick when she grabs my hand and we walk out. On the drive over, I begin to feel worse and almost pull over to puke. *Get a grip, Wilder. You have to do it so just fucking do it already.*

*But, you don't have to,* a little voice whispers. I'm not sure if it's the angel or the devil or Auntie Rita I hear, but it is true. I can turn the car around, drive Harlow back to the apartment and make love to her all night long. Angelo has no idea where I'm staying and it would take him a while to track me down.

I can go into the ring the next ten fights, hopefully win and have the money to pay him back. I know Jax would give me the money, but I refuse to ask him. He's bailed me out of bad situations before and I won't drag him into this. He needs to focus on his new bride, not his bum of a brother.

This is my problem and I need to take care of it myself.

My choice is simple: hand over Harlow in an hour or die.

I need to stop thinking Angelo Savini will grant me any more reprieves. He's made it clear he wants to question Harlow and even if I handed him ten grand on a silver platter right now, I think he'd still have his goons break my legs.

When we step through the large doors of the Velvet Room, I automatically reach for Harlow's hand, lacing my fingers through hers. I look around for anyone who seems suspicious, but all I see are a lot of happy, drunk, high club goers.

If I didn't know better, it almost feels like we are on a date.

The club walls are draped in swags of dark red velvet and the air thumps with some trance-like song. A fog machine clouds the atmosphere every so often giving the place a dream-like quality. And, being here with Harlow, holding her hand, I feel like I am in a dream.

I'm trying to scope the place out when she pulls me toward the dance floor.

"C'mon," she says. "I haven't danced in forever."

"I don't dance," I tell her and dig my heels down, pausing at the edge of the crowded floor.

"Not even with me?" she asks and makes a pouty face.

I lean down, brush her hair back from her ear and place a kiss there. "Why don't you dance for me?" I whisper.

Harlow lets go of my hand and sashays backwards, getting swallowed up in the sea of dancers. I stand there, cross my arms and watch as she moves to the music. Her hips sway and she lifts her arms up, finding the beat of the song.

*Christ.* My breathing increases and my entire body grows hot. I can't tear my eyes off her. Watching her body move to the music, head thrown back, hips lilting. It's mesmerizing.

All I want to do is take her home.

Then, some douchebag comes up behind her, trying to dance with her. Something inside me snaps and I stomp over, yank her toward me and narrow my eyes at the dude. "She's with me," I growl.

With a sexy smile, Harlow slides her arms around my neck, moves up against me and guides my body into rhythm with hers. We couldn't get closer if we tried and I love the feel of her curves pressing down the length of my body.

I rest my hands on her hips, enjoying how they move from side to side and undulate against me. Thoughts of last night infiltrate my head and I remember how well we moved together then, too.

Like we were made for each other.

Her hands slide back around and then she pulls my face down to hers and kisses me. *So fucking hot.* It's deep and desperate and there's a lot of tongue involved. My hands glide down and move over her perfect ass, pulling her into me even closer.

I'm hard as hell and her scent is driving me crazy. Vanilla, a touch of sandalwood and, of course, strawberries. She tastes like red wine and torta barozzi, the cocoa-coffee flavored cake we ate for dessert.

The fog machine fills the air as Harlow starts kissing my neck and all I want to do is fucking leave. Take her home with me. I'm on the verge of doing just that when I spot a couple of tough-looking guys at the bar. Particularly, the southwest corner bar adjacent to the emergency exit.

*Fuck.*

Is it midnight already? I reach into my pocket and pull my phone out. 12:02am. It feels like acid fills my stomach.

"We need to go," I say and pull back from her roaming lips.

She looks up at me with passion-glazed eyes and I swallow hard. *God, she trusts me.* The realization hits me hard and fast. How in the hell was I going to hand her over to a snake like Angelo Savini?

"Where?" she asks and runs a hand down my chest.

"My place?" I ask and reach for her hand, pulling her into the crush of dancers and moving away from the men at the corner bar.

She giggles, trips and I catch her. And, she looks up at me with such wide, innocent blue-gray eyes that my heart catches. "I'd like that," she says. "But, I think the exit is that way."

"Well, we're going to go this way," I say, redirecting her. I glance over my shoulder and don't see Angelo's men. *Shit.* Where did they go? I wrap my arms around Harlow, pulling her in front of me and propelling her through the endless dancers.

I see a dark hallway not far away and hope there's a door at the end of it. Finally, we escape the throng on the sweaty dance floor and I grab her hand and hustle her toward the hall.

"You're sure in a hurry," she says with a chuckle.

We start down the hallway and she has to jog to keep up with me. I spot the red glowing exit sign at the end and move toward it. I don't anticipate someone grabbing my shirt, hauling me backwards and then tossing me into the wall.

The air whooshes out of me when I hit the brick, scraping my cheek. I spin around to see one of the big guys who was waiting at the bar. If he wants a fight, I'll give him one. "Go!" I yell at Harlow. Then, I haul my fist back and slam my knuckles into his jaw, making sure my rings make contact. I don't have brass knuckles, but my chunky rings are the next best thing.

The guy falls back and then charges forward, taking me down in a tackle. As I go down and hit the floor, I realize Harlow is still standing there. "Harlow, go!" I grit out and dodge a meaty fist. I slam my knee up, catching him in the groin, and twist sideways.

And, that's when I hear Harlow scream my name.

She's near the exit, caught in the second man's arms. *Fuck.* I start to run toward them and then feel about 280 pounds slam into my back and take me down.

"Motherfucker," I hiss after my chin hits the ground. I ram my elbow back as hard as I can and hear something crack when it makes contact with his face. As I scramble away, I see blood all over the place and realize I must've broken his nose. But, I don't bother to look.

I take off down the hall, but don't see Harlow or the other guy any more. He must've dragged her outside. I plow through the exit door, launching myself into the air and catch a glimpse of him trying to stuff her into an SUV.

But, my girl is feisty and I can't help but smile when I see her kick his shin. He cries out and I grab his jacket and swing him around. He flies through the air, drops and I land a kick in the center of his chest. As he falls back, I grab Harlow's hand.

"C'mon!" I yell and we take off running down the alley.

"What the hell is going on?" she asks, her long legs keeping up with mine.

But, I don't say anything, just keep us moving fast until we reach the Range Rover. We jump in and I slam the car into drive. Eyes pinned to the rearview mirror, I hit my foot down on the gas, swerve the wheel and leave the Velvet Room in the dust.

# 13

## HARLOW

I spin in my seat, hand against the dash, and look at Bastian with wide eyes as he drives like a maniac. "Who were those guys?" I ask. My earlier buzz is gone, replaced by fear and confusion.

"Are you okay?"

My shoulders relax when he slows down a little. "Yeah, how about you?" It's dim, but I can see his cheek and chin are scraped. And, his knuckles. But, they're always messed up from fighting.

"Fine," he mumbles.

"Did you know them?"

"Not exactly," he answers carefully.

*He knows something,* I think. "What's that supposed to mean?"

"I know one of them. They're a couple of Angelo Savini's guys."

"Who's that?"

Bastian lets out a long sigh and rakes a hand through his hair. "You're not going to like what I'm about to tell you. But, I'm done lying."

My heart sinks. *He's been lying to me?* I fucking knew it was too good to be true.

"I don't know exactly how to tell you this."

"Just tell me the truth, Bastian. Please."

He pulls the car over, puts it in park and turns, studying me closely. "Not long ago, I ended up owing this guy named Angelo a lot of money. I placed some bad bets and ten grand later, I had no way to pay him back."

I listen carefully and so far nothing he says surprises me. Or alarms me. I know Bastian's been involved with all sorts of shady people and activities. "Go on," I say.

"I thought I could pay him off by fighting. If I win, I can maybe make a grand on a good night." I pause, swipe a hand across my scraped-up knuckles. "The night we met, I won the top cash prize. Defeated some guy named Tiger who didn't take it too well. It wasn't a normal fight, though, because we had to use knives."

"Oh, my God," I whisper.

"Anyway, he followed me over to Platinum Security, attacked me and stole the cash."

Suddenly, it all comes together and I remember hearing the scuffle, the broken front door and Bastian laying on the sidewalk with a knife wound. "So, you knew your attackers?"

He nods. "I said I didn't because I didn't want to upset Jax. I also didn't want a lecture." His gaze meets mine. "It also gave me a reason to talk to you."

"And, now you don't have enough money to pay this Angelo back?"

"Right. So, he made me an offer."

"Which was what?" I ask. A wave of unease passes through me.

His gaze drops and his hands tighten into fists. "See, this is where I really wanna lie."

"Tell me the truth, Bastian." I lay a hand over his and he looks into my eyes and I know I'm not going to like what he says. "Please."

He sighs, but holds my gaze, flips his hand and laces his fingers through mine. "Angelo offered me a deal. He'd forgive my debt if…"

I wait for him to tell me, but he clams up. Then, he swoops in over the console and captures my mouth in a kiss. I part my lips, slide my tongue along his and moan. God, he knows how to kiss. I'm glad I'm sitting or my knees would buckle.

After a heated moment, I pull back. "He'd forgive your debt if what?" I ask, refusing to let him distract me any further.

"If I brought you here tonight and gave you to his men."

My jaw drops and I pull my hand away. "*What?*" It's like someone just dumped a bucket of ice water over my head.

"I barely knew you when he told me what he wanted," Bastian hurriedly says. "And, he made it sound like no big deal. He just wanted to ask you some questions."

"About what?" I ask, my head spinning. What in the world do I know that would interest some criminal?

"I don't know. But, maybe he needs you to hack into something?"

"Then, he could've fucking hired me! Not abducted me from a club," I say, starting to get angry. Who did this guy think he was? And, the fact that Bastian was going to just hand me over to him like nothing had happened between us cut me deep. Really, really deep.

God, why am I so stupid? Why had I trusted him? I feel so betrayed.

"I'm so sorry, Harlow." When he reaches out, I pull away. "Fuck. I never planned for this to happen."

"For what to happen, Bastian?" I snap.

"For *us* to happen."

But, I just shake my head, reach for the door handle and yank it open. "There is no us, Bastian," I say and feel the prick of tears. "There never was."

I slide out of the car and take off.

"Harlow! Wait!"

But, I ignore him and keep running. We're close to Jax's apartment which means we're pretty close to mine. When I hear the Range Rover move up beside me, I glance over and the window is down.

"Harlow, please, talk to me," Bastian says.

"I have nothing to say to you."

"I know I fucked up. Bad. I wish I could say I was this perfect stand-up guy, but I'm not. I'm a first-class fuck-up who never does anything right. I suck, Harlow, I know that. Everyone knows that."

I stop walking and look over at him. "So, change." He blinks as though he's never considered the possibility. "In the meantime, leave me alone."

I hurry away, leaving him to mull over my words. I mean, really, it doesn't take rocket science to figure it out. If you're not happy with your behavior, work on changing it.

God, I feel so utterly let down. The last person who made me feel like this was my Dad. Big surprise that he and Bastian are so similar.

*You knew this, Harlow.* You fucking knew it. So, why are you so surprised that the underground fighter covered in tattoos turned out to be a bad guy? Turned out to be a man you couldn't trust.

My feet click along the pavement and I ignore the Range Rover that continues to follow me. At least, he's smart enough to not try and talk to me anymore. Because I am done. Men like Bastian are "what you see is what you get" and I know this. God, I could just kick myself.

I fell for his charm, his whispered lies. *Freckles this, strawberries that.*

*You're an idiot, Harlow.* You may be a genius when it comes to computers and hacking, but when it comes to men, you don't know your ass from a hole in the ground. So pathetic.

I am so done. From this moment on, I'm swearing off all men. Especially Bastian Wilder. I'll just be single, keep my distance from the opposite sex and focus all of my attention online where no one can hurt me.

Because, let's face it. The fact that the man I just slept with, was intimate with, lured me to a nightclub like a sheep to the slaughter and then planned to throw me to the wolves breaks my heart on every level.

*Bastard.*

I guess I mean nothing to him.

In less than ten minutes, I unlock my front door and glare at the Range Rover that followed me to make sure I got home safely. I step inside and slam the door shut with all the force I can muster.

Then, I sink back against it and finally let the tears fall. God, I feel so fucking betrayed. Here I am, falling so hard for this man, and he's plotting to hand me over to the bad guys.

I was just a pawn to him, I realize. After he made that deal, I'm sure he set out to seduce me and gain my trust so it would be that much easier to trick me later. And, I fell for it. Hook, line and sinker.

*You, idiot.*

I might be upset and angry with Bastian, but I am absolutely furious with myself for knowingly falling for a man that's way too similar to my Dad. I knew this would happen. *Fucking knew it.*

From the first time I looked down into his hazel eyes, my gut said Bastian Wilder was nothing but potential heartbreak and bad news. And, now here I am crying so I shouldn't be surprised how this all turned out.

I swipe the tears away and steady myself. I see mascara on the back of my hand and sniff. *Who am I?* I think. Wearing all this makeup, all dressed up for some man who doesn't give a shit about me. Drinking too much.

God, this is exactly why I lose myself in my work and computers. They'll never hurt me.

I push away from the door and head to the bathroom where I wash my face and brush my teeth. Then, I drag myself over to my bedroom, strip off my clothes and pull a clean, oversized t-shirt over my head.

With a heavy heart, I fall onto my bed and burrow beneath the blankets. *What could this Angelo want from me?* I wonder. I rack my brain, mentally reviewing all of my latest work, our cases and clients. Ever since Columbia, things have been pretty above-board.

For the most part, anyway.

So, I don't think anyone is coming after me because they're angry or out for revenge. And, if the guy wanted me to do a job, he could've simply hired me. So, what do I know? Why in the world would some criminal think I possess some kind of information that would be useful?

Other than hanging out on the Dark Web, I don't consort with bad guys. Hell, the only shady character in my life, other than the guys at P.S., is my Dad who I never see.

*My Dad.*

I sit up, drag my laptop over and open the email he sent me earlier. I re-read through it, paying close attention to the part where it gets weird and makes no sense: *But, avoid men who seem too sparkly, too loose to be true. And, definitely avoid Antwerp over Valentine's Day. Even if it's the love of a century.*

He's trying to tell me something, I realize. Maybe even warn me?

But what?

I pull up a search engine and type in Antwerp and Valentine's Day.

And, get a million hits on the Antwerp diamond heist.

"Holy shit," I say and click on the story.

Dubbed the "heist of the century," it was the largest diamond heist and one of the largest robberies in history. Thieves stole loose diamonds, gold, silver and other types of jewelry valued at more than $100 million. It took place in Antwerp, Belgium, in 2003 over Valentine's Day weekend.

*Okay, Dad, you have my attention. Question is, what are you trying to tell me?*

Is he referring to the diamond heist he pulled? Warning me to avoid men "who seem too sparkly, too loose to be true."

God, that sounds like Bastian.

Whatever my Dad's trying to say, I get the feeling it's a warning.

I hit reply and my fingers shake above the keyboard. I squeeze my hands tightly and take a deep breath. Here goes nothing, I think, and begin to type a response to my Dad.

I haven't seen him in over five years, since he's been in prison, and I'm beyond nervous. But, what choice do I have? These bad guys want something and I need to go to the one man who will most likely know.

My father.

# 14

# BASTIAN

The days pass and all I can do is admit that I screwed up yet again. I spend some time feeling sorry for myself then angry because Harlow won't pick up when I call. And, when I text, her response remains the same: Leave me alone.

I sink into this dark depression, my feelings alternating from anger to sorrow to worry. I don't leave Jax's apartment and I drown my sorrows in a combination of alcohol, cigarettes and fast food.

And, I remember how happy I was for a brief amount of time--since the moment Harlow found me bleeding outside of Platinum Security and I looked up into her blue-gray eyes. Something about her entranced and intrigued me like no other woman has managed to do before. It's almost like we were kindred spirits. I told her I thought we were a lot alike.

I still believe it.

Harlow makes me feel things that I honestly didn't think I had in me. Or, if I did at one time, they are long dead or dormant now. She gives me a genuine feeling of joy that has been missing from my life for a very long time.

I guess that's what happens when you lose people you love. That flame of hope inside you slowly goes out. Being a ten-year-old boy and having both parents die in an accident left me confused and angry. I had a lot of pain inside me and I didn't know how to deal with it or what to do. Jax and Maddy dealt with it in their own ways and I rebelled.

It was hard for me to express the hurt and angry feelings. I never talked to anyone so I had to resort to other outlets. I pulled away from my siblings and found myself drawn to all sorts of trouble. Jax was a troublemaker, too, but not like me. I was the worst kind of kid because I didn't feel bad about anything.

Through it all, Jax still managed to maintain a conscience. A human aspect to himself that I inevitably lost. I hung out with the worst kids, all from broken homes, and I wasn't scared to do anything. Except face my own brokenness.

I would take on any challenge, any dare and I was a firm believer in trying anything and everything at least once-- alcohol, drugs and finally sex. I was the first one to jump, fight, steal or lie despite the consequences. Now, looking back, I realize it was because I felt so completely empty, devoid of normal feelings and emotions, and I desperately yearned to feel something, anything...even if it was bad.

While Jax and Maddy dealt with their anger and heartbreak over our parents' death, I shoved mine aside and ignored it. They found other things to focus on like school and friends while I pushed everyone away. Eventually, Jax decided to become a cop and he threw himself into that goal 110 percent.

Poor Maddy didn't live long enough to become anything other than a statistic. *Fuck.* My heart breaks when I think of my vibrant sister shot down by drug dealers. And, then it grows cold and crystallizes with ice when I think about how I used to hang out with those assholes.

I mean, they weren't exactly my friends, but we did run in the same circles and I knew who they were and how they found out Tony Zerillo, Maddy's boyfriend, was skimming off the top, pocketing money from dealing their shit.

The second I heard that, I should've run straight to Jax and told him. But, I didn't. Honestly, I didn't think twice about it because Tony got picked up for dealing and the cops threw his dumb ass in jail. I figured it was a blessing in disguise because now he was away from Maddy. Ironically, it was always okay for Jax and I to be bad boys, but when my sister started to date one, we were not pleased.

I guess because we knew better than anyone how terrible guys like us could be. Unreliable, selfish, insincere. The stigmas and stereotypes are all true.

It never occurred to me that those guys would go after Maddy to teach Tony a lesson. That they would break into her apartment and gun her down without any hesitation or remorse. I know she called Jax when they were trying to get in, when they were breaking down her door, and he ran over there to protect her. But, he was too late. By the time he got to her place, the deed was done and he found Maddy in a pool of blood on the bathroom floor.

July 7.

The date she died is embedded in my mind and heart. Inked on the backs of my fingers so I can look down every day and be reminded how I failed her. A form of self-punishment, I guess. Because, I should've stepped up and said something. I should have found a way to save my sister.

After her funeral, I did what I do best and I took off. The guilt hit me hard. Not only because I failed her, but because I saw what it did to Jax. Jesus Christ, I'd never seen anyone so torn apart and consumed in guilt. He blamed himself because he got to her place too late. I blamed myself because I kept quiet and now had to see him crumble.

Jax was always so strong and my rock. My anchor no matter what happened. So, when he lost it, I had to leave. Witnessing my big, tough brother fall apart left another hole in my heart that I didn't want to face or deal with.

That was a year ago and I haven't been back since. I wandered around aimlessly, searching for something. Some kind of closure, peace maybe? I spent some time in Las Vegas, indulging in carnal pleasures and pursuits. Trying to drown my sorrows in women and alcohol. I gambled more than I should have and lost way too much.

Then, I drove my bike up more North and explored Utah. The

natural wonder and beauty of the state soothed me. I drove all over Arches Natural Park, absorbing the sheer beauty of the stunning stone arches and rolling petrified dunes, backed by the snow-capped peaks of the La Sal Mountains.

Then, I explored the brightly-colored and tightly packed hoodoos that dominate the landscape at Bryce Canyon. The stone pillars, glowing in shades of orange, cream, pink and cinnamon jutted up from the floor of the huge natural amphitheater and I would just sit there, smoke a cigarette and absorb the beauty all around me. The magical landscape helped take the edge off like the women and booze couldn't.

With no destination in mind, I followed cliffs, plateaus and the Colorado River. I think my favorite spot was Grand Staircase-Escalante National Monument. It's a huge area of rugged terrain dominated by canyons, arches, hills, waterfalls, forest and scrubland. There's a sense of remoteness on those dirt roads and you can drive great distances without ever passing another vehicle.

Trick is, you have to be happy with your own company and even though the natural beauty all around me was stunning, it couldn't fill the holes in my soul. It couldn't give me what I needed to allow me to forgive myself.

After nearly a year of wandering and avoiding Jax's calls, he left me a message saying he was getting married. And, he asked me to come home for the wedding. I'll never forget how he sounded in that message-- there was a lightness in his voice that had been absent since Maddy's death. True happiness radiated through my phone and I became damn curious about the woman who was able to help him out of the black suction of guilt and despair.

I've yet to meet Easton Ross, but she must be one hell of a special lady. Because she managed to save my big brother when no one else could and because of that, I'll be grateful to her forever.

My mind inevitably turns back to Harlow. God, I feel like such a shit and I want to talk to her. Try to explain things better. But, really, what is there to explain? I tried to save my ass by sacrificing hers. The more I think about it, the worse it sounds.

At least, at the very last moment, I did the right thing. I got her out of the club and made sure she got home safely. That's something, right? Sad and pathetic, typical Bastian, but something. At least, I try to tell myself it is.

Then a dark thought occurs to me: is she safe?

*Fuck.* I sit up straight on the couch and hope to God that Angelo didn't track her down. I know he's called me a few times, but I just ignore it when Unknown Caller pops up. He's probably ripping the city apart looking for me and I know it's only a matter of time before he finds me.

And, I don't even care. Break my legs, shoot me, whatever. At this point, maybe it would be best to just put me out of my misery like some wounded animal. Let's face it, I'm about as worthless as they come and everyone would be better off without me.

But, that doesn't make me any less worried and I decide I'm going to drive by Harlow's. Even though she's done with me, I need to make sure she's alright. It's the least I can do.

But, then I hear a knock and a key turn. The door opens and Jax walks in looking tanned, relaxed and well-rested. "Hey," he says and steps inside. "Didn't look like you were home." He glances around and frowns. "Why's it so dark in here?"

Jax opens the blinds and sunlight streams inside. I blink and look away like a vampire. He turns, takes one look at me and tilts his dark head. "What's wrong?" he asks. "You look like shit."

"Thanks," I mumble and run a hand through my hair. God, I need to wash it.

"Are you hungover?" he asks and looks down at all the empty beer bottles and trash on the coffee table.

I shake my head. "No, but I'll probably start drinking soon."

"What the fuck, Bastian?" He sits down on the couch and looks over, studying me with his "cop" look that can detect bullshit a mile away.

No point in lying because he will know. "I fucked up," I say.

Jax lets out a breath and prepares himself for the bullshit storm that he knows is coming. "Do you need money?"

"Yeah, but I think it's too late for that."

"What do you mean?" he asks.

I tell him about Angelo Savini and the money I owe him. About gambling, about the underground fights and how that's the reason I wound up stabbed outside of Platinum Security. "But, it gets worse," I say. "I dragged Harlow into it."

Jax's dark eyes narrow. "What?" The calm, happy, relaxed vibe he came in with earlier disappears and now he hunches forward, elbows propped on knees, and lines forming at the corner of his eyes.

"Angelo said Harlow has information he wants. Last night, I was supposed to hand her off to a couple of guys at a club and then Angelo was going to ask her some questions. But, I couldn't do it, Jax. Even to save my own ass, I couldn't give her to them."

"Why not?" Jax asks in a quiet voice. But, he already knows. I can see it in his eyes.

"Because I'm falling for her."

"Oh, man." Jax runs both hands through the long hair on top of his head and releases a breath. "How did that even happen? Last I knew, she was supposed to drop you off here and that's it."

"Yeah, well, that wasn't it. We ended up spending more time together," I say carefully.

But, Jax is too keen. "You slept with her, didn't you?"

"Just...the one time," I admit.

Jax rolls his eyes and sighs again. "I'm gone for *one* week. *That's it.* And, look what happens."

"I care about her," I insist. "And, you know me. I don't care about anybody. Not even myself."

"So, what's that mean? You want a relationship? Or, another romp in the sack?"

*A relationship?* I pinch the bridge of my nose, waiting for the fear and urge to run to strike. Oddly, it doesn't. "I don't think it matters what I want. She's pissed and won't talk to me." He raises a brow. "Because I told her everything last night."

"You told her the truth?" he asks, voice full of disbelief.

"Yeah. I mean, I figured I owed it to her. Besides, I'm done lying."

For a long moment, Jax doesn't say anything. Then, a sly smile curves his mouth. "Who are you and what have you done with my brother?"

I give a half-snort, half-laugh and shake my head. "Good question."

"So, Harlow won't talk to you, huh? Maybe it's time to do some groveling."

"I can grovel. Not sure it's gonna work, but, at this point, I have to try." I stand up and start pacing. "God, I can't stop thinking about her. It's driving me insane."

Jax chuckles. "Wow. I never thought I'd see the day Sebastian Wilder would fall for a woman."

"Was it this complicated when you and Easton got together?"

"Yeah, you could say that. I was supposed to be protecting her from a stalker and all I wanted to do was-"

He abruptly cuts off, but I get the point.

"How was the honeymoon?" I ask.

A dreamy, satiated look passes over his face. "Perfect. Before Easton, I never thought I'd be this happy. After Maddy died, a part of me died. I was so focused on revenge, so caught up in the dark and the guilt. But, Easton changed all that."

"I'm happy for you, Jax. Really happy that you were able to make peace with everything that went down." I wish I could find my own closure. Maybe if I let Jax know the truth...*Jesus.* What is it with wanting to be honest all of a sudden?

I stop walking back and forth and drop down on the arm of the couch. "How did you do it? I mean, I know you said Easton helped, but how?" I ask.

"She made me realize that Maddy's murder wasn't my fault."

"That's because it was my fault," I blurt out.

"What are you talking about?"

I slide down off the arm and sit down on the couch cushion, rubbing my fingertips against my temple. "I never told you this, but, I, um, at one point associated with the assholes who killed Maddy. I should've been here when shit went down. Tried to help you stop them. But, I wasn't and..." My throat closes up. God, I miss my sister.

"Bastian, it wasn't your fault. It was Tony Zerillo's fault. That scum she was dating had a rap sheet a mile long. When those gangbangers went after Maddy it's because they couldn't reach Tony because his dumb ass was in jail."

"I know, but I still feel terrible. For what you went through, too. And, I just took off. What the hell kinda brother am I?" I reach around and rub the back of my neck. "Not a very good one. It's why I haven't been able to come around since she died. Too much guilt."

"I think it's time to let it go," Jax says.

I let out a shaky breath. "Easier said than done, right?"

"You just have to do it. It's not easy, but it helps if you have a goal or maybe someone to focus your attention on. Like Harlow."

"I'm not gonna hold my breath."

"Everybody screws up. You...just more than most," he adds with a half-smile. "I want you to find happiness, like I did, and I'll help you. With Harlow, with a job, with whatever you want."

For the first time since I can remember, I feel a surge of hope. Maybe Jax is right. "I've actually been giving a lot of thought to cleaning up my act. Figuring out what I'd be good at and finding a legit job. I mean, better late than never, right?"

"What're you thinking? A career in retail or the fast-food industry?"

I flip him off. "Actually, I've always been interested in detective work." I wait for him to laugh, but he doesn't.

"Why don't I set you up with Logan Sharpe? He and I worked on the force together and now he's a LAPD detective."

"Yeah, that would be great, thanks."

"He'll probably try to dissuade you from doing it, but you never know."

"You know me. Takes a lot to change my mind once it's set on something."

Jax eyes me closely. "Is it set on Harlow?"

"Yeah, definitely," I say without any hesitation.

"Then I'll help you."

"Thanks, bro." I sigh and remember how mad she was at me. "I'm gonna need it."

"Don't worry, you'll figure it out. And, if you're serious about getting your shit together then good things will start happening for you. I know it."

I nod, feel a smile curve my mouth. I hope he's right.

## 15

# HARLOW

I'm nervous as hell as I wait in the large waiting room to see my Dad. The man who skated in and out of my life and probably doesn't even know my birthday. I look around, wipe my sweaty palms against my jeans and check out the other prisoners and visitors.

They all seem happy to be visiting, enjoying each other's company, looking completely at ease while my stomach churns and heart races. I've basically ignored Robert Vaughn the past five years. I have no idea if he's going to be mad, hold a grudge, be difficult. Or, if he will actually be happy to see me.

I sit at a table in the corner, not wanting to draw attention to myself, eyes on the doorway that my Dad will walk through. It takes maybe ten minutes before he appears and I stand up, watching his blue eyes scan the room and then land on me.

Those eyes, bluer than mine, crinkle up at the edges when he smiles at me. He looks at ease and wears a blue chambray shirt and light denim jeans. As he gets closer, I can see how gray his hair is now and it gives him a more distinguished look, but he's still as tall and handsome as I remember. When he reaches the table, I don't know what to do.

"Hi, sweetheart," he says. I haven't heard his gravelly voice in so very long and it does something funny to my heart. Despite all of our ups and downs, it suddenly hits me that I have missed my Dad.

"Hi, Dad." I sit down because there's no way I'm hugging him. Besides, you're only allowed limited contact with prisoners. He sits across from me and folds his hands on the tabletop.

"It's so nice to see you." He shakes his head, unable to stop smiling, and this look of wonder crosses his face.

"What?" I ask, feeling uncomfortable under the weight of his stare.

"You've just grown into such a beautiful and intelligent young woman. I have a hard time believing I contributed to that in some way."

"I'd say other than genes, you didn't contribute all that much."

My words come out harsher than I intend and he shifts in his seat. "You're right. I don't deserve any Father of the Year award."

"Look, Dad, I'm not here for a social call. I came here because I'm hoping you can shed some light on a situation," I say, getting right to the point. "There's a man who seems to think I have information about something-- I have no idea what-- and he tried to kidnap me the other night. And, after that strange email you sent, I'm wondering if the two are connected?"

"Smart girl," Robert says. "I knew you'd figure it out."

"I haven't figured anything out. Especially why some crook like Angelo Savini is interested in me."

A dark look crosses his face and then he sighs. "Aw, shit, Harlow. I screwed up."

His words hit me hard, but it's Bastian's voice I hear saying them. God, they are two peas in a fucking pod. "What did you do, Dad?"

He taps a finger on the table and finally looks back up at me. "Savini was in here with me for the last two years. I should've kept my mouth shut, but the kid was on my nerves. Bragging, thinking he ran shit around here and that he was better than me because he was young and I'm just some washed-up old man. I wanted to put him in his place. Let him know he was a rookie and I was a vet. So, I told him about my final heist. How I did it and what I got away with."

"Oh, Dad," I say. "What were you thinking?"

"Now, he wants to know where I hid the cache of diamonds. And, he's thinking you either know or can find out."

"Shit," I swear. "Between you and Bastian, I swear to God! Why am I surrounded by men who lie and deceive me?"

"Who's Bastian?" he asks in a quiet voice.

"Nobody. Just some asshole who tried to sell me out to Angelo."

"Honey, I'm sorry. I didn't know-"

"You're always sorry! If I had a nickel for every time I heard that-"

"You'd have a dime."

It was an old joke he and my brothers used to say. But, I can't even summon up a smile much less a chuckle. Because he foolishly bragged to a fellow inmate about having a hidden cache of diamonds, I have to deal with it now.

"So, where are these diamonds?" I ask in a tired voice.

He looks around the room then leans forward and lowers his voice. "They're safe. My partner has them."

"Partner?" This is the first I'd heard of my Dad having committed the heist with a partner.

He nods.

"So, you're saying you took the fall and never gave up your partner's name?"

"Never. I may be a lot of things, mostly bad, but I'm loyal as the day is long."

"Who was this partner?" I ask.

"It doesn't matter."

"Doesn't it bother you that you're locked up in here and he's out there probably spending all that money and living the good life?"

"Nah. Because that's not what's happening."

"How do you know?"

"Because my share of the diamonds is in a safe place. Until I get out."

"You really think so Dad? Because that sounds naive," I say and shake my head.

"If you have trust, you have everything."

I narrow my eyes. When did he become so philosophical? I wonder. He's probably attending some Christian inmate program. "If you say so. But, where does that leave me? What am I supposed to tell Angelo?"

"The truth. That you have no idea where the diamonds are and that you and I have no relationship left."

His words make my gut twist. This isn't how I wanted things to end up. Just like every other little girl, I wanted my Dad in my life. But, he's the one who chose to leave. Not me. And, here we are-- our relationship nearly non-existent.

Suddenly, I feel really sad.

"Do you really think Angelo will believe me when I say I don't know where the diamonds are?"

"It's the truth."

"Just tell me where they are."

"I don't know where they are."

Frustration slams through me. "You just said your ex-partner has them."

"Right, but I have no idea where they're hidden."

"You're a liar," I say. "I hope you can sleep at night knowing you chose those diamonds over your daughter." I push up and glare down at him. "Thanks a lot, Dad. Once again, I can't count on you."

"Honey-"

But, I throw my hand up and stomp away. I don't want to hear another word from him.

Because he's breaking my heart.

On the drive home, part of me is devastated and the other part of me isn't surprised at all. The fact that my Dad didn't tell me where his share of the diamonds is just reinforces my belief that he's a selfish man who only cares about himself.

Tears threaten, but I refuse to cry over someone who doesn't give a shit about me. After the rollercoaster of emotions passes, I just feel really, really sad. And, my mind turns to Bastian.

The fact is, when it came down to it, Bastian didn't hand me over to Angelo. He sure waited until the last damn second, but he ended up doing the right thing. He pulled me out of that club and then he told me the truth when he could have easily lied.

In all honesty, I'm the one who lied.

*I'm so sorry, Harlow...I never planned for this to happen.*

*For what to happen, Bastian?*

*For us to happen.*

*There is no us, Bastian. There never was.*

But, I know that's not true. Because something happened that's never happened to me before. I developed feelings for a man. I guess that's why I keep running away from him. The idea of caring for a man who has a history of taking off and a self-proclaimed fuck-up terrifies me.

I mean, when *he* says he's bad news, then only a fool would fall for him.

Apparently, I'm that fool.

The first night we met, Bastian said he thought we were a lot alike and I'm beginning to believe that. Lately, I've been doing an awful lot of lying and running. So, who am I to judge him so harshly when I'm behaving in a similar fashion?

By the time I reach LA, it's early evening and I go straight to my apartment even though I'd like to go to Bastian's. I still don't know how he feels, hell, I barely understand my feelings at this point, and I want to talk to him, but I have things to do.

No knight in shining armor is going to sweep in and save the day so I need to save myself.

Once I'm settled down in front of my computer, black coffee steaming in my mug, I slide my glasses on and get to work. It's time to discover what really happened five years ago. I crack my knuckles and focus on the large monitor in front of me.

My Dad had a partner in the heist. This is news to me and the police kept that little tidbit under wraps. Even though I should probably try to keep things above board and call Logan Sharpe over at LAPD, I don't have the luxury of time. So, I run a backdoor program, bypass the firewall and silently slip into the LAPD database.

Once inside, I move around, searching through various files like a silent wraith. A ShadowWalker. No one will know I'm in and they certainly won't realize I'm looking through any information regarding Robert Vaughn and a diamond heist that occurred over five years ago.

*Jackson Palmer.*

The name jumps out at me because I've never heard it in association with my Dad. According to the detective report, Jackson Palmer, 57, of Beverly Hills, provided valuable intel to Robert Vaughn when he worked at The Beverly Hills Hotel, the location where the heist occurred.

Apparently, the Saudi Arabian prince was staying in a suite at the luxury, five-star hotel, located on Sunset Boulevard and Palmer conveyed the prince's itinerary to Vaughn, noted his comings and goings and provided an array of items such as gate and key cards, a hotel uniform and even an adjoining suite.

Palmer basically gave my Dad the tools he needed to waltz in, steal the diamonds and waltz out.

It would've been successful, too, if the prince's mistress hadn't shown up unexpectedly and witnessed my Dad sneaking out. She testified against my Dad and Palmer got off for lack of evidence. Conveniently, Jackson Palmer is also the brother of one of Hollywood's top producers. I'm sure quite a few favors were bestowed and palms greased.

After all, the old saying "it's all who you know" isn't just a Hollywood thing. It works in all areas of life and I guess it kept Palmer Jackson out of prison.

So, my Dad took the entire blame and Palmer rode off into the sunset with his half of $10 million in diamonds. I leave the LAPD network and drop into a deep search on Jackson Palmer. Currently, he lives in a $3 million mansion in Beverly Hills and doesn't work.

Of course, he doesn't work. He's living off the sale of the diamonds. And, nothing appears suspicious because his brother is worth $80 million plus.

I jot down Palmer's address and decide to pay him a visit. Only thing is, I should probably have back-up. As I consider my options, I know there's only one person I want having my back and that's Bastian.

# 16

## BASTIAN

After Jax leaves, I feel really good about our talk. For the first time in my life, I have a goal. Two goals, actually. Number one: get my girl back. And number two: find out if I want a career as an investigator.

I need to find Harlow and start groveling. This may just be my biggest fuck-up to date so I know it's not going to be easy, but I have to try. Because if she's feeling even half of what I'm feeling then she'll listen to me. I know it.

It's time to clean up and make myself presentable. I'm not going to score any points when I smell like a stale booze joint. I clean up all the crap from the last few days of feeling sorry for myself then hop in the shower. I shave, suds myself up and then gargle enough Listerine to set my mouth on fire.

Afterwards, I dry off, wrap the towel around my waist and throw some mousse in my hair. It's too long to spike up on top, but the sides are shorter, and the mousse just helps keep it out of my eyes.

As I splash on some of the woodsy aftershave I like, I hear a knock at the door. Maybe Jax came back to start packing because he's moving in with Easton now. I head out and throw the door open.

And, my heart slams into my ribs when I see Harlow. Her gaze drops and I forget I'm just wearing a towel. "Sorry," I say. "Just got out of the shower."

She drags her eyes back up and I motion her inside.

"I'm glad you're here. I was about to come find you," I admit.

"Really? Why?"

"Some things I wanted to tell you," I say, my voice suddenly raspy because I'm nervous as hell.

"That can wait," she says. "Right now, I need your help." Her tone is all professional and I instantly recognize she's on a mission.

*She needs me.* "Yeah, sure, anything."

Her gaze dips down again. "Do me a favor and get dressed. We're going to Beverly Hills and I don't think they'd appreciate you walking around in that thin towel."

My mouth edges up and I give her a nod. "Have a seat. I'll be right back." I head down to my room, slip into a black t-shirt and jeans. I yank a pair of boots on and my leather jacket. Then, I head back up the hall. "Why Beverly Hills?" I ask.

Harlow stands up. "I'll explain everything on the ride over."

Harlow doesn't explain much of anything on the way over and now I'm more curious than ever. She simply says there's a man she needs to talk to and that I'm to act as her muscle in case he gets physical.

"Who is this guy?" I ask again.

"Jackson Palmer."

"You told me his name, but who is he exactly? Why do you want to talk to him and why the hell do you think he might hurt you?"

Harlow sighs. "I can't answer all of your questions right now, Bastian. Honestly, I don't have any answers, anyway. That's why we're here." She pulls the SUV over to the curb and narrows her eyes. "His house is the third one on the left."

The place is big and the expansive lawn in front must be watered by a sprinkler system three times a day to keep it that green. Harlow reaches for her tablet and pulls a beanie down over her head. For the first time, I realize she wears all black and my pulse kicks up a notch. "Are we breaking in?" I ask.

"If you ask me another goddamn question, I'm going to punch you," she says.

Damn, I love it when she gets all spicy. I close my mouth and follow her down the palm tree-lined street. Instead of going to the front door, she motions for me to duck behind a tall hedge with her. Then, she lifts her tablet and her fingers fly.

I want to ask what she's doing, but I know she's hacking into something. Besides, I don't want to get punched. The light from the screen glows on her face and it's clear that she's in her element. I watch, mesmerized, at how fast she types. How she knows exactly what she's doing and the confidence in those steel-blue eyes. She's beyond impressive and it turns me on.

"House alarm is deactivated as well as perimeter property intruder alerts." She tucks the mini tablet inside her jacket and looks up at me. "Ready?"

"Hell yeah," I whisper, my adrenaline hitting.

Harlow gives me a smile. "C'mon."

We make our way toward the back of the property, sticking to the shadows, staying low. There's a tall gate and Harlow tries to open it. "Locked," she whispers.

"No problem," I say.

I motion her over then drop down and make a basket with my fingers. She steps onto my clasped hands and I boost her up. Harlow grabs the top of the gate, swings over and drops down. When she's safely over, I leap up, grasp the wooden slats and heave myself over, landing on bent, crouched legs.

"You should really consider working at Platinum Security," she murmurs and I feel my mouth edge up. "You'd fit right in."

A part of me thinks I'd really like that. Working with Harlow and the guys every day.

Once we're in position in the yard and have a clear view of the back of the dark house, I wait to see what our next move will be. Harlow removes her mini tablet and goes to work again. A moment later, she glances up at the dark house. "One heat signature inside," she says. "Upstairs, left side of the house."

After tucking the tablet back inside her jacket, she zips it up and looks over at me with a determined look. "Let's go."

We jog across the shadowed yard and stop at a back door. Harlow pulls a key and small screwdriver from a different pocket. "Bump key," she murmurs. "Courtesy of Griff."

I watch closely as she slides the bump key into the keyhole and then taps it with the screwdriver. This forces all the tumblers inside the lock above the shear line and, in that split second when the pins are in the perfect position, she applies a little torque in the right direction and the lock pops open.

"Damn," I whisper. "Less than 20 seconds."

She slips the tools back inside her pocket, gives me a sly smile, and pushes the door open. I stay close, on her heels, and we find the staircase and start up. At the top, we head left, moving down the hallway, and pause before a partly-closed bedroom door where a light glows inside.

I see Harlow take a deep breath, then step forward and push the door all the way open. I follow, ready to act as her muscle or go down fighting. Whatever she needs.

A man sits on the edge of the bed, scrolling on his cell phone when we walk in on silent feet. His graying head jerks up and his mouth drops open in surprise. "Who the hell are you?" he asks, looking from me to her.

"My name is Harlow Vaughn and I have a few questions for you, Palmer."

His eyes widen when she says her name. "Robert's daughter?" he asks, his voice nearly a whisper.

"That's right."

"You could've called, you know. Instead of breaking and entering." He looks at me and I cross my arms and stand up straighter, doing my best to look intimidating. "Who's this?"

"My associate," she says. "In case you try to make a run for it."

But, Palmer just shakes his head. "My days of running are over, honey. I also was never very good at hiding, either. Too much stress and anxiety."

"You sure seem to hide behind your brother," she remarks in a dry voice.

"Touche." Palmer sits back on the bed, tosses his phone aside. "Ask whatever you want. I probably owe you an explanation, anyway."

"I want to know where the diamonds are," she says, tone firm.

*Diamonds?* I try not to look surprised, but wonder what the hell she's talking about.

But, it's clear that Palmer knows exactly what she's talking about because he doesn't hesitate with an answer. "After the heist, we split them up. As you can see, I bought a house and some fun toys with my half. I have no idea where Robert stashed his cache."

"Bullshit," she says.

"It's true." He shrugs.

"He told me that you have them."

Palmer frowns and a confused look passes over his face. "Why would he tell you that?"

"He said his share was safe and that his partner had it," Harlow insists.

"First of all, Robert is smart. He would never go away for 10-15 years and leave his take with me. I'm not that trustworthy."

Something wavers on Harlow's face. "I said the same thing," she admits in a low voice. "I told him he'd be naive to trust you. Especially after you left him hanging out to dry."

Palmer shakes his head and sighs. "I didn't have a choice. I did what my brother said. Otherwise, I'd be in an orange jumpsuit, too."

"Blue," Harlow mumbles.

"Whatever," Palmer says and waves a hand through the air. "Neither is my color. The point is, he took his half and I took mine. And, I haven't seen him since that night at the Beverly Hills Hotel."

Harlow seems to be considering his words. "There's not a third partner, right?"

"What? No."

Her question generally seems to confuse him so it seems like she buys his answer.

"Fuck," she hisses. "Then where the hell is his share and why would he say it is with you?"

"I wish I had the answers, kid, but I don't. Besides, these are probably questions you should be asking Robert."

"I already did," she snaps. Harlow heaves a frustrated sigh out and glances at me. I can see the turmoil of emotions roiling in her pretty eyes and I get the urge to draw her into my arms and comfort her.

But, now is not the time.

"Well, I guess that's it then," Harlow says. "Again, you've proven to be quite useless, Mr. Palmer." As she turns to leave, Palmer sits up straighter.

"How did you get past the locks, alarms and sensors?"

"Easily," she comments in a dry voice and walks out.

Back in the Range Rover, Harlow rips the knit cap off her head and hits the steering wheel with a fist. "Sorry for dragging you over here, but I had no idea how he was going to react."

"No problem. Whatever you need, you only have to ask."

She drops her head back and sighs again. "I really thought he had them."

I want to ask her a million questions, but her mood is volatile and my gut says to hold off. That she'll come around when she's ready. Other than an occasional, annoyed sigh on her end, the trip back to East Hollywood is quiet.

When we roll up to Jax's apartment and I should get out and leave, I can't. My ass feels glued to the seat. And, then we both start talking at the same time and abruptly stop.

I need to let her know I'm not the horrible person she probably thinks I am. I need her to understand that making that deal with Angelo eats me up inside and, when it came down to it, I'd never give her up to him. Would never let him hurt her.

"You first," she says.

"Will you come in? For a minute?"

"Why?"

"I have some groveling to do."

But, she shakes her head. "I don't really want to see you grovel, Bastian."

"Okay, then, let me explain a few things. Please, Harlow."

She lets out another weary sigh. "Fine," she relents and turns the car off.

*Thank God,* I think. I need her to understand. To forgive me.

We get out and head up the small walkway. I pull out my key then slide her a sideways glance. "Guess I know who to come to if I ever get locked out."

Her mouth curves up and it's the first smile I've seen from her all night. "I'm still learning," she says. "Griff is the real lockpicking expert."

"I don't know. Looked like you knew what you were doing to me."

"What can I say? I'm a good student."

As we walk inside, I peel off my jacket. "Sit with me." She follows me over to the couch and visions of our last time on this couch together flood my mind. It's where we had our first kiss and I don't think I've been the same since. The moment I tasted Harlow Vaughn, I knew I had to have more. She makes my entire body sing.

God, I just want to drag her into my arms.

But, I can't. I have to make things right first.

*Yeah, okay. Here goes nothing.* "Harlow, I don't know what you're thinking-- except that maybe I'm the biggest asshole you've ever met-- but, this is all really new and it scares the ever-living fuck out of me."

I take a deep breath and look into her steel blue eyes. "I've never been in a relationship longer than two nights. I'm unsteady, unpredictable and completely unworthy when it comes to someone like you. But, I want to change all that. I want to try to be a better man. For me, for Jax...for you."

With baited breath, I wait for her to tell me to fuck off. I deserve it. But, something flickers in the depths of her eyes and she reaches out and lays a slim hand over mine. "Bastian..." Her eyes slide shut. "I know I should stay away from you, but...God help me, I can't."

"I know I'm not good enough-"

"Why don't you think you're good enough?" she interrupts.

Her question throws me. But, I vow never to lie to her again. "I'm not very good at making the right decision. Even when I try, I usually mess things up. Look at Jax's wedding-- he almost missed the flight for his honeymoon because of me."

I flip my hand over and move my fingers through hers. "I was always a screw-up with no direction. Ever since I was a kid. And, I just accepted it. But, now that I see how Jax, Griff and Ryker all got their lives back together, it kind of gives me hope that I can, too. Here's the thing-- I never had a reason to try until you."

When her eyes fill with tears, I reach out my other hand and grasp hers. "Why're you crying? Shit, I'm messing this all up."

"No, you're not," she says and squeezes my hands. "I'm just a mess of emotions tonight. But, you're doing a really good job."

"Don't cry," I say and wipe her tear away with the edge of my thumb. "At this point, I feel like I messed it up beyond repair with you, but I hope you'll still be there. As a friend, I mean. Maybe kinda help me take those first few steps getting my shit together?" The last thing I want is for her to feel like I'm cornering her into a relationship if she's not interested.

I'm not exactly sure what flashes through those beautiful, stormy blue eyes of hers, but her arms wrap around me and her lips press to my ear. "I never want to be just friends with you, Bastian," she whispers. "I want so much more than that."

*She wants me.* I pull back so I can meet her gaze. "You do?" It's like music to my ears, but a part of me still can't believe it. Fairytales and happy endings just don't happen for a guy like me. At least, they never did before this amazing woman came into my life.

Damn, I think getting stabbed and falling back into her arms was the best thing that ever happened to me.

She nods, places her hands on either side of my face and then leans in. Our mouths meld together and relief pours through me. God, she tastes like heaven. If heaven were covered in fresh strawberry patches.

Desire spikes through me and I want this woman more than the air I breathe. I shove my hands through her thick, dark hair, angling her head back so I can deepen the kiss. Our tongues meet and mate, fast and furious, and I can't get enough of her.

I'm thinking the feeling is mutual because we both start tearing each other's clothes off. Naked and trembling, I scoop Harlow up and carry her down to my bedroom. Our mouths never break apart until I lower her down onto the bed.

"Who'd guess you were so traditional?" she teases. Then, she yanks me down and straddles me. "Lay down," she says and pushes a hand against my chest.

Flat on my back, I look up and watch her begin kissing her way down my chest. "Traditional, huh? We'll see about that," I say as that tongue of hers swirls over my tattoos, tracing the ridges in my abs, and then drops and dips to circle my navel.

Her tongue traces the "X" below it. Then, she glances up at me and quirks a dark brow. "X marks the spot?" she asks.

I freeze, hands tightening around her hips, and when her fingers wrap around my cock, it's pure bliss.

"Fuck," I hiss as she strokes and pumps and licks until I'm on the verge of blowing.

But, I have other, more non-traditional plans. I'm going to make this last and I'm going to give her the most intense orgasm of her life.

I pull her hands away, moving them behind her back. "Don't move," I tell her and then reach back around to return the favor. My fingers slide through her folds and she moans when they circle around her clit and discover just the right amount of pressure to make her cry and writhe her hips.

I sink my fingers inside her and toy with her until she's right on the verge. Then, I stop. Her eyes snap open and she makes a small, disappointed noise in the back of her throat. "Don't stop," she begs.

I flip her around and pull her up onto her hands and knees. Her long chestnut hair spills down onto the mattress and the sight of her on all fours in front of me, that delicious ass in the air, makes me hard as steel. I drop forward, my cock pressing against her rear, and whisper into her ear, "I'm going to take you right to the edge and stop. And, then I'm going to do it again. And, again. Until you can't stand it any longer." I nip the back of her shoulder. "And, when I'm done, you're going to scream my name and come harder than you ever have in your life."

A shiver runs through her and I reach over, grab a condom and roll it on. I move in closer, splay a hand on her shoulder to steady her and begin to slide into her hot, wet body. Harlow pushes that delectable ass back, grinding against me, and I shift her up and reach around to find her swollen nub.

When I can't go any deeper, I slide back out, then in again, starting a slow, steady rhythm. "Faster," she urges me, slamming back. But, I grip her hips with one hand and continue to tease her with the other. "Oh, God, Bastian, *please*."

"Easy, freckles," I say. "I already told you we're going to go slow. So...fucking...slow." I trail my tongue up her spine and when I feel her body begin to clench and tense, it feels so good, but I pull out. I want to keep edging with her, pushing us both to near climax and starting over to increase the pleasure, but it's getting too hard.

"Bastian-" Her voice sounds desperate.

I flip her onto her back and look down into her passion-glazed eyes, panting, knowing neither of us can handle much more. I kiss her hard and the moment I feel her begin to relax, I slide back inside her, drawing her leg up and slow and easy gives way to fast and hard.

"You're so tight," I rasp, thrusting, pounding, driving into her now. All my earlier control disappears and she wraps her legs around my waist, moving with me and, at the same time, holding on for dear life.

"Bastian!" she cries and arches up. Her orgasm slams into her hard and a hoarse cry rips from her throat. She arches her long, slim neck back and when she comes, I've never seen anything so beautiful.

A second later, the pressure building at the base of my spine explodes. Pleasure vibrates through my entire body and it's nearly unbearable it's so good. I shudder and drop down with a groan.

When I finally catch my breath, I lift my head and stare at the gorgeous woman beside me.

*I'm falling in love.*

The feeling is completely new, but strangely, it's comfortable. I'm not scared. I want this woman in my life. Always.

Harlow Vaughn is everything I've secretly wanted, but never had the guts to actually pursue. The possibility of rejection hovers at the back of my mind, but I think we're on the same page. I hope, anyway.

"That was so good, but so..."

"Traditional?" I ask and run a finger down the slope of her nose. "God, I love your freckles." I lean in and pepper kisses over them. Her cheeks lift with a smile and she runs a hand through my hair, pushing it off my face.

"More like torture," she says.

"Sweet torture," I correct.

"What am I going to do with you?" she asks.

"Whatever you want," I tell her. "I'm all yours."

I guess she wants to kiss me because she drags her lips over mine.

*Mine.* That's exactly what she is and I couldn't be happier. *All mine.*

# 17

## HARLOW

*This man is going to be my undoing.* No doubt about it. But, he's taking me on the ride of a lifetime and I'm feeling things that I've never felt before. I let out a sigh and snuggle up against his warm chest. He nuzzles his face in my hair and we both doze off.

When I wake up a couple of hours later, it's probably because Bastian's warm lips are moving over my neck and it tickles. I laugh and pull back. "You're better than an alarm clock."

"Sorry, I couldn't resist."

I make a soft humming sound in the back of my throat as he continues to lick and suck. Then, I trace a finger along his upper arm and the skull inked there. "Why a skull?" I ask.

"Because one day we all die."

"That's a pleasant thought."

"It's true. Some sooner than others, but, eventually, it happens to everyone."

"Do all of your tattoos have some meaning?"

"Of course."

"Tell me." I point to the cross.

"That one's for my Aunt Rita. She was a God-fearing, Bible-thumper and I miss her sermons."

I smile and kiss the cross. "I think I would've really liked her." My hand glides over the large black and white rose on his shoulder. "And, the rose?"

"My Mom's favorite flower. She had a garden full of them-- all different colors-- and she and Maddy used to cut them and fill vases all over the house. It smelled so good in the summer."

Emotion tightens my chest and I brush my lips over the flower. For a bad boy, Sebastian is incredibly sensitive. I lower my finger to the pair of dice etched above his wrist. "Because you like to gamble?" I ask.

"Because life's a gamble. Some days you win, some days you lose."

I lift his arm and drag my lips over the dice, my eyes trained on his hazel ones, and I feel him draw in an unsteady breath.

"You gonna kiss every one?" he asks, voice husky.

"Eventually," I say. The green-eyed panther on his forearm always intrigued me and I place an open-mouthed kiss against it.

"Black panthers are solitary animals. People rarely see them in the wild and they're the 'ghosts of the forest.' They're mysterious, powerful and do their own thing."

"And, you've certainly got the green eyes in common."

He shrugs, watching as I press my lips to the nautical symbol on his side. "What about the anchor?"

"Reminded me of Jax. Strong, dependable, a port in the storm. If you need him, he's always there. And, I've needed him quite a few times."

"He's a good brother."

"Yeah. Too bad he got me in return."

"Don't say that. We need to work on your self-esteem." I lift my hand and touch the cursive letters that spell out Madison on his chest. "And, of course, this is for you sister." I kiss the ink over his heart.

"It's hard to believe she's been gone a year and a half now. Sometimes it feels like she was here just yesterday. And, other times, it feels like I haven't seen her in forever."

"I wish I could've met her."

"You guys would've gotten along great. She was always so full of life, always joking and laughing. When Jax and I lost her...it gutted us."

"I'm so sorry." I lift his hand and press my lips to the *0707* on his four fingers.

"Such a waste, you know. So fucking unfair."

"I know," I whisper. "But, that's why you have to remember the good things. To keep her memory alive. That's what she would want."

He points out the checkered racing flag on his arm, not seeming to hear me. "Know why I got this one? Because I run. After Maddy died, I couldn't get away fast enough. I'm always moving, trying to get as far away as I can. But, I'm like a race car on a track and I keep circling back around. Never making any true progress."

I lean forward and drop a kiss over it. "Because this is home. You keep coming back because your family is here."

As he considers my words, I slide my mouth down to the infamous "X" below his navel. "And, this one?" I ask.

"The letter X symbolizes a lot-- a warning, a crossroads, a kiss..." His voice trails off and he inhales swiftly when I place a heated kiss there.

"Are you trying to warn me off?" I ask, a teasing note in my voice.

"Never," he says.

Bastian is excellent at distracting me, a perfect escape from my "Daddy Issues." But, at this point, it has morphed into so much more than that. He gives me hope.

He makes me believe that we have a chance together. A future.

And, I've never had that feeling before.

"Earlier, you said you never had a reason to try until me," I say. He pulls back and looks at me, his hazel eyes intense. "I've never tried either. I always ran from love and relationships. It was so much easier just hiding behind my computer."

"Are you saying you wanna be in a relationship with me, freckles?" he asks with a teasing smile.

I nod and feel a flush heat my face. "I'm saying I want to try. If you're game?"

"Oh, I'm more than a game," he says. His lips capture mine is a slow, sensual kiss and everything feels perfect. Except for the fact that my Dad didn't care enough to choose me over a handful of diamonds.

Bastian lifts his head and studies me closely, sensing something is off. "What's wrong?"

God, he can read me well. "I didn't want to tell you this now-"

"Tell me," he says, his gaze serious and so very intense.

I sit up and lean against a pile of pillows, tugging the sheet up under my arms. Bastian stretches out beside me like a big, lazy cat, not caring that the sheet barely covers him, all of his attention on me. He scrunches a pillow beneath his chest between his propped elbows and waits for me to continue.

"So, the man whose house we broke into tonight and then questioned is Palmer Jackson, my Dad's ex-partner. When we talked about my family before, I mentioned my Mom and brothers. But, not my Dad." He nods and, as if he can sense how hard this is for me to discuss, he reaches over and laces his fingers through mine.

"You said he smokes. That's it."

I take a deep breath. "A little over five years ago, my Dad went to prison." I wait for him to tense or pull away, but he doesn't do either. He just waits for me to go on. "He was a career thief and a very good one until he got caught stealing some diamonds. I thought he had pulled the job by himself, but no. I just found out about Palmer. My Dad went to jail and Palmer's rich-ass, famous producer brother got him off without a hitch. No one knows where my Dad's share of the diamonds is hidden. It's like they disappeared. People assumed he sold them, but I don't think so."

I take a deep breath. "Yesterday, I visited him at the prison for the first time. I hadn't seen or spoken to him in over five years. He had sent me this weird email. It seemed like a warning and after everything that happened with Angelo, I got the feeling my Dad knew something that I didn't. That even you didn't."

I shift on the bed. "I hoped he could help clear things up," I continue. "He told me that he was locked up with Angelo Savini for awhile." Bastian's entire body tenses. "Savini pissed him off so my Dad bragged about the heist and that the authorities never found the diamonds."

"Shit."

"Yeah. So, Angelo must believe that I know where they are and my Dad-" *Dammit.* My voice catches in my throat. "My Dad wouldn't tell me. All he said was he gave them to his old partner to hold for him until he gets out. So, I did some digging in LAPD files and found Palmer Jackson's name and connection to the theft."

"And, he claims he has no idea where your Dad's share is stashed."

I nod, feeling a huge wave of frustration, disappointment and anger crash over me. "I'm so pissed at him, Bastian."

"C'mere," he says, sitting up. He pulls me into his arms, against his chest, and his large hand strokes down my face, dipping into my hair and toying with it. "I'm sure that wasn't easy. Seeing him after all that time."

I shake my head. "No. And, then he lies to me."

His lips press against my temple. "Are you sure he knows?"

"Of course, he knows. He can deny it until he's blue in the face, but the one steady constant about my father is he's a liar. No doubt about that."

"What exactly did he say?"

"When I asked him what I'm supposed to tell Angelo, he said to tell him the truth. That I have no idea where the diamonds are and that he and I have no relationship left." I let out a hurt sigh and squeeze my eyes shut. I absolutely refuse to waste one more tear on that man. "He's such a bastard. But, I can't say I'm surprised. He was never there for me and only came around when he wanted something."

Bastian gets quiet and I can't help but wonder if he has the capacity to change. Because my Dad sure didn't.

"This is why you scare me," I whisper. "I see so many similarities between you two."

"Harlow, I'm not your Dad," he says in a low voice. "And knowing you think we're so similar makes me want to change even more. I won't let you down. I promise." He tightens his arms around me and tugs me close.

I want to believe him more than anything. But, a part of me is still skeptical. Despite that, I'm going to give him the benefit of the doubt and trust that he's going to give me his all.

"I'm here for you and I'm not going anywhere. Okay?"

"Okay."

"We're not going to be able to hide from Angelo forever," Bastian says. "I think we need to come up with a plan."

"Like what?"

"For starters, talk to your Dad again. Make him tell us where his share is stashed. I know Angelo and he's not going to give up until he has the diamonds in his hands."

"He wouldn't tell me, Bastian."

"I'll go with you and help persuade him."

For a moment, I don't say anything. "You'll go with me?" I ask, not expecting the offer.

"Of course," he says. "Don't worry. We'll come up with a plan to keep you safe."

"Okay. I'll schedule a visit," I tell him and he places another kiss against my temple.

The next day, I find myself in the California State Prison waiting room again. But this time, Bastian sits with me. I have no idea how this is going to go and when I see my Dad walk through the doorway, my nerves kick up a notch.

Bastian must notice how I tense up because he reaches over and covers his hand with mine. "You got this," he says under his breath.

My Dad looks from me to Bastian and then down at our clasped hands as he pulls out the chair and sits. "I have to admit, I was surprised you wanted another visit after the other day." His blue eyes assess Bastian closely. "I take it you're Bastian?"

I can tell he's surprised my Dad knows his name, but Bastian plays it off and offers his hand. "Sebastian Wilder," he says.

"Robert Vaughn." They shake hands. Under normal circumstances, I'd be happy they're meeting, but this is a far cry from the normal father meeting his daughter's new boyfriend scenario.

"Dad, you said your old partner was holding the diamonds for you.

Well, I talked to Palmer Jackson last night and he claims he has no idea where your share is and that he never had them."

His blue eyes darken. "Palmer Jackson. That's a name I haven't heard in awhile. Rat bastard."

"He flipped on you and got away scot-free. Why the hell would you even consider giving him your half?"

For a long moment my Dad doesn't say anything and I feel my patience slip. "I don't know where the diamonds are, honey, but I do know they're safe."

I pull my hand out of Bastian's and slam it against the table. As my anger bubbles over, Bastian shifts beside me, knowing that I'm about to lose my shit. "All you do is lie to me! First you say you don't know where they are. Then you say your old partner is keeping them for you until you get out. What's the truth, Dad?" I ask, my voice rising. "Don't you care that I have some mafia gangster on my ass, trying to kidnap me? Threatening me?"

I want to cry until I feel Bastian's hand slide over my knee. It gives me strength, reassures me, and, in this moment, I feel so much love toward him. And, from him. It's pouring off him in waves and a calmness settles over me.

"I know you don't understand, but the diamonds are safe," my Dad says again.

"How could you possibly think that?" I ask in a tired voice. "Or, trust someone who let you take the fall?"

My Dad takes a deep breath then spreads his hands on the tabletop. "Harlow, when I said my ex-partner, I didn't mean Palmer Jackson."

I frown, not understanding.

"I'm referring to Marina Lopez who is...hell, you could call her a former girlfriend, an ex-lover, an old partner...whatever. The point is, after the arrest, I made sure she had the diamonds and she promised to keep them in a safe place for me."

*An ex-lover? Oh, God.* "I had no idea you had someone else in your life," I murmur.

"I didn't want you to know. Hell, I was still scared to tell you just now." He lifts his hands and gives me a crooked smile. "You're a firecracker when you're pissed, kiddo."

I think I see Bastian's mouth curve, but I don't say anything. I'm still shell-shocked that my Dad had a significant other, for years, that I knew nothing about it.

"I didn't tell you out of respect for you and your mother. I know you blame me because things didn't work out with us."

"I blame you because you left Dad. You walked out on me, Dane, Rafe *and* Mom."

"I'm sorry, sweetheart. I never meant to hurt you and your brothers. It was hard for me to come after and visit, but make no mistake--I never stopped loving my children."

I swallow hard, happy to hear those words, but not completely convinced that they're true.

"Yeah, well, actions, Dad. They speak a lot louder than words."

"I know and I'd like to start showing you. Will you give me that chance?"

Beneath the table, Bastian's hand tightens over my knee. As if he's telling me that whatever my decision is, he will support me. I drop my hand beneath the table and lace my fingers through his.

"I can try," I whisper. "But, I need you to try, too. I need you to try really fucking hard, Dad."

"I will, sweetheart. I promise."

I pull my thoughts back to the problem at hand. "What makes you think Marina didn't sell the diamonds and skip town?" I ask. I have a hard time believing that any woman is going to hang around, hiding a bag of diamonds for 15 years, until Robert Vaughn gets out of the pokey.

"Because she visits me every week, honey."

My eyes widen. "*What?*" Wow. He sure never had time to visit me and my brothers, but sounds like he and Marina spend plenty of time together. Even when he's in jail.

Before I can get upset again, Bastian speaks up. "Mr. Vaughn, it's only a matter of time until Angelo tracks Harlow down. We're going to come up with a plan to keep her safe and eliminate the danger, but if you can give us any information that will help us, we'd appreciate it."

I look over and admire how confident and composed Bastian is because I feel like I'm about to crumble. He squeezes my hand and I'm so grateful he's here with me.

"If you want to know where the diamonds are then you'll need to ask Marina. I can let her know you're coming. She owns a flower shop in North Hollywood and you can meet her there."

"Thank you," Bastian says.

I begin to simmer down when my Dad gives us the location of the shop and makes it sound like he doesn't care if she tells us where she hid the stolen diamonds.

For the first time, I think he's telling me the truth. He has no idea where the diamonds are. "You really don't know where they are, do you?" I ask

He shakes his head. "No, honey. I have no idea. And, truthfully, I don't care."

That snags my attention and a frown furrows my brow. "Why not?"

"I never really cared about the prize. It was always about the challenge and succeeding."

"Maybe," I say. "But, I still don't understand how you can trust her."

For a moment he doesn't say anything. Then, he smiles and runs a hand through his silver-tipped hair. "Because she's the love of my life. And, love makes you do crazy things."

# 18

# BASTIAN

After meeting with Harlow's father, we sit down on a bench outside and I give her a minute to regroup. I can see how hard it is for her to deal with her Dad and the whole Marina bomb didn't help. "You did good in there," I tell her and run a hand up and down her back.

Harlow lets out a breath. "You kept me together when I probably would've fallen apart or stormed out like last time. Thank you for that."

"C'mere," I say and pull her into my arms. She rests her head on my shoulder and it feels good. Knowing that I was there for her. I've never really been around when anyone needed me before.

"So, what's the plan?" she asks and looks up at me.

"I think it's time to bring in reinforcements. Fill in Jax and the other guys. They'll know what to do."

"I think you're right," she agrees.

"Between me, a former cop, Navy SEAL and CIA op, we'll keep you safe," I say.

"Yeah," she says with a smile. "I think I'll be in good hands."

"No doubt about it," I say and then brush my lips against hers.

We make good timing back to Los Angeles and before going over to the Platinum Security office, Harlow wants to stop by her place and grab her laptop. I pull up to the curb and she jumps out of the Range Rover. "Be right back," she says. I watch her walk away and get the feeling she puts an extra little swing in her hips just for me.

With a smile, I lean back into the seat and wonder how I got this amazing woman. Harlow Vaughn is good for me. She makes me take a closer look at myself and she doesn't accept any of my bullshit. She doesn't let me accept it, either.

She challenges me in every way and keeps me on my toes. I love that. And, let's not forget that she's the most stunning woman I've ever seen. Her long dark hair, steel-colored eyes and breathy voice leave me a little short of breath. And, don't even get me started on her freckles.

And, God, she's exactly what I need in bed. Willing, expressive and so very passionate. Definitely *not* vanilla.

*I'm not going to fuck this up.* Harlow is the best thing that's ever happened to my dumb ass and I'm going to figure out how to get Angelo off our asses and keep this woman in my life. At this point, I wonder how I ever lived without her?

A few minutes later, I'm watching a girl walk her dog down the sidewalk when I realize it's taking Harlow a long time to grab her laptop. I glance down at my Dad's watch and, suddenly, something doesn't feel right. I get out of the car and head up the walkway to her apartment.

As I reach for the door handle, a bad feeling washes over me. I push the door open and step inside. "Harlow?"

No answer.

Everything looks normal and I head down to her office. "Harlow?" I call, my voice louder.

When she still doesn't answer, I feel the first wave of panic hit me and break into a jog. But, she's not in her office. Or, her bedroom, bathroom or any other part of the apartment. *Fuck me.*

*Where the hell is she?*

That's when my phone rings. Unknown Caller.

I swipe the bar and lift the cell up to my ear. "Hello?"

"Oh, Bastian. You didn't deliver the girl like you promised so I had to come and get her myself. And, it really pisses me off when someone tells me they're going to do something and then they don't. Like pay off their debt."

My eyes slide shut. Angelo has Harlow. A cold, oily feeling curls low in the pit of my stomach. *How did I not see them leave?* I wonder. But, when I feel the breeze move through an open window, I know.

*Fuck, fuck, fuck.*

This is all my fault. Well, mine and Robert Vaughn's. God, Harlow is surrounded by men she can't depend on and I feel awful.

"So, here's the deal," Angelo says. "You still owe me 10K, motherfucker. I'm going to get the answers I need from her...and then I'm going to start torturing your woman. And, I'm not going to stop until you pay every last dime."

His voice drips with dark, excited anticipation and I can tell he's getting off on the power he wields over me. For now, anyway. Because I'm going to track his ass down and get Harlow back if it's the last thing I do.

"I can get you the money, Angelo. Right now. From my brother. Give me an address and I'll bring it over."

"Nah, I wanna play with her first," he says in a low, ominous voice.

My heart sinks. If he lays one finger on Harlow, I'm going to kill him. "You touch her, you die," I warn him.

Angelo laughs. "Am I supposed to be worried? I mean, when do you ever keep your word, Bastian?"

"I swear to God, I'll kill you," I grit out and clench my hand into a fist.

"Just get the money. After I ask Miss Vaughn a few questions and get to know her a little better, I'll call you with further instructions."

"Angelo-"

Click.

"Fuck!" I yell and throw the phone into the couch cushion. I shove my hands through my hair and, for the first time in my life, I'm scared I'm going to let someone down. Terrified that I'm going to fail Harlow.

I jog back down to the Range Rover, jump inside and call Jax. I fill him in as quickly as possible and tell him I'm headed over to the office. He stays calm, the voice of reason, always an anchor, and that helps me pull my shit together, get my emotions under some semblance of control.

"Griff and Ryker are here. We'll figure this out and get her back, okay?"

"Okay," I say, trying to suppress the panic.

"Just keep it together and get over here."

The drive over is excruciating despite the fact that it's only a few minutes long. My mind churns with nightmarish images of Harlow and Angelo. He's a sick fuck, I think, and I underestimated him. I didn't think he was much more than a hood who ran the local gambling circuit. Shit, I couldn't have been more wrong.

The idea that I came so close to tossing her to him like some kind of fucking bone makes me hate myself.

I have to find her before he hurts her. Before it's too late. Before something terrible happens that will cause me to never be able to forgive myself.

Harlow is supposed to be the one to help me find the light. Not be the reason I condemn myself to the shadows.

When I walk into Platinum Security, they're all down in Jax's office and when I storm inside, I must look like a wild-eyed basket case. I'm so overwhelmed and panicked that Angelo is going to hurt Harlow that I can't even think straight. Thank God for these three.

"Hey," Jax says, eyeing me closely. "Calm down, Bastian."

I nod, slide a shaky hand through my hair. I feel like a junky, jonesing for my next hit, but I have no idea how to get it. I'm going crazy with worry, on the verge of losing it. "I'm trying."

"Who is this asshole and when did he take Harlow?" Griff demands, blue eyes flashing.

"Angelo Savini and maybe 15 minutes ago. I was in the car while she ran into her place to get her laptop. But, she never came out. They were inside waiting."

"And you owe this guy money?" Ryker asks.

"Ten grand. But, there's more to it than that."

"Yeah, Jax told us about her Dad and the diamonds," Griff says and scrubs a hand across his bristled chin.

"According to her Dad, only one person knows where the diamonds are-- his girlfriend Marina Lopez."

"And, this Marina owns a flower shop, you said?" Jax crosses his arms.

"In NoHo."

"So, that's where they'll go," Ryker says.

"Angelo wants the diamonds, but from what he said, he also wants to get back at me for not handing Harlow over to him earlier. He's going to hurt her," I say, my voice cracking.

"Motherfuck," Griff swears.

"We're going to assume a couple of things," Jax says. "One, that Angelo Savini is more interested in getting his hands on the diamonds than Harlow. And, two, that Harlow will tell him Marina is the only one who knows where they're stashed and they head straight to her shop."

"So, what's the plan?" Ryker asks. He pulls his Sig Sauer out of its holster, ejects the magazine, checks it and slams it back into place.

"We go in hot," Jax says. "That means we strike fast and get Harlow out. I'm not fuckin' around with this guy and I don't want him coming back around after any of us. That means we're going to use some intimidation tactics."

"Looking forward to it," Griff says and pops a stick of gum.

Jax nods. "Bastian you'll get Harlow out while we have a little talk with Savini."

"He'll probably have a couple of his men with him," I say.

"I'll take care of them," Ryker says.

I let out a pent-up breath and I'm so grateful that these guys are on my side. We're going to get Harlow back. We have to because otherwise, I'm going to lose my shit. Like permanently.

"Do you need a piece?" Jax asks me as he tucks his Glock in the back of his waistband.

But, I shake my head. "I'm better with my fists," I say.

Griff reaches into his boot and pulls a folded knife out. "Even so, better have something," he says and tosses me the tactical knife.

I catch it and slip it into the back pocket of my jeans. Unlike these guys, I don't wear cargo pants with a hundred pockets where I can stash my endless supply of weapons. Or have holsters for guns and sheaths for blades. I fight with my fists, my speed and my wits.

I feel a hand on the back of my shoulder and look over at Jax. "We've all been there. We'll get her, bro. Just hang in there a little longer."

I have complete faith in Jax, Griff and Ryker. They take the term badass to a whole new level. We just need to get to Harlow in time.

As we head out to the Range Rover, I look up to the sky and, for the first time since I was ten years old and my parents died, I say a little prayer.

*Please, watch over Harlow and keep her safe.*

# 19

# HARLOW

My eyes flutter open and I try to reach a hand up to touch my pounding head, but I can't. I glance down and realize I'm tied to a chair with zip ties. *Shit.* I pull and only manage to make the plastic cut into my skin.

*What the hell happened?* The last thing I remember, I left Bastian in the car and ran into my place to grab my laptop. But, I didn't even reach my office. Halfway down the hall, a big guy stepped out of my bedroom and then someone came up behind me and must've knocked me out because everything went black.

I look around, not sure where I am. Some kind of a warehouse, maybe? It's big with a concrete floor, brick walls and shelves full of junk. There are a few high windows, but they're up near the ceiling, completely out of reach.

I twist my wrists, trying to loosen the zip ties, when a man appears. A man who can only be Angelo Savini. As he walks over, I size him up and I'm not overly impressed. He's on the short side and has a mafia look about him-- well-dressed, gold rings, dark hair that's slicked back. His black eyes drop down, moving from the top of my head, downward, lingering in certain areas a bit too long, and I shift in the chair, growing uncomfortable fast.

"I can see why Bastian likes you," he says in a silky voice. "Still, we could have avoided this if he just handed you over at the club."

My eyes narrow and I grit my teeth together. I want to tell him to go to hell, but I have a feeling that I should keep my mouth shut for the time being and not aggravate him.

Angelo stops in front of me, leans down close and looks me in the eye. "I'm torn," he says.

I don't shrink away or show any sign of intimidation. "What are you talking about?" My voice sounds strong and sure and I look him in the eye.

"See, I had every intention of getting the information I needed out of you and then leaving. But, hell, Harlow. You're a hot piece of ass. Maybe I shouldn't be in such a hurry, after all."

Hot dread pours through me. The idea of this scum touching me makes me sick. "I'll tell you whatever you want to know," I say.

When Angelo runs a finger down the side of my face, his touch makes me flinch. I can't help it. "I want to know why you're with a loser like Sebastian Wilder," he says. "Is he that good a fuck?"

"He's a good man," I grit out.

A nasty laugh erupts from deep in Angelo's throat and he stands back up straight. "He's a waste of space. A complete fuck-up who would sell his own mother out for a few bucks."

"That's not true," I say. *God, I hate this guy.* And, he doesn't know anything about Bastian.

"He almost sold you out. Guess some prime pussy made him change his mind at the last minute." His oil-slick eyes move down my body again.

I bite the inside of my cheek, knowing I need to get him focused on something other than me. "I visited my Dad," I tell him.

That gets his attention. "Ah, good 'ol Bobby Vaughn. How's the old codger holding up?"

"Fine. He mentioned you."

"I'm sure he did. I always got the feeling he didn't quite think I measured up to his lofty standards. I mean, the man was the best thief around at one time. But, then he got old and slipped up."

"He may have been caught, but they never found the diamonds," I remind him.

"Which is why you're here. I want that stash and you're going to tell me where he hid it."

"He didn't hide it," I say. "He gave it to his ex for safekeeping."

"His ex?" I hear the disbelief in his voice.

"That's right. She hid the diamonds and no one knows where. Not even my Dad."

"Bullshit."

"It's true. Apparently, she's the love of his life." When he raises a brow, I shrug. "Yeah, it was news to me, too."

"So, who is this mystery woman?" he asks.

I don't want to throw Marina Lopez under the bus, but Bastian knows about the flower shop. If he wants to find me then that's where he'd go. I just know it. "Her name is Marina and she has a flower shop in North Hollywood. If you want the diamonds, she's the only one who can tell you."

Angelo eyes me for a moment and must reach the conclusion that I'm telling him the truth. "Let's go for a ride," he says.

*Thank God. Oh, Bastian, please go there,* I think, trying to send him a mental message.

It doesn't take long to get to the small shop and on the ride over, I run through different escape scenarios. Angelo's got two of his thugs with him, though, so now I have to ditch him and his two goons.

They also have guns and that makes me nervous. Jax and the other guys might sleep with a gun under their pillow, but Bastian doesn't. Bastian is more street and fights with his fists and wits.

Angelo heads toward the front door and one of his muscle men grabs my arm and yanks me with them. A closed sign hangs on the door and I'm happy no one is here. But, of course, that doesn't stop them from breaking the lock and shoving the door open.

No alarm sounds and we go into the shop. It's a decent-sized place with endless potted plants, displays of trinkets on shelves, a counter with a cash register and two coolers full of fresh cut flowers. Angelo makes his way behind the counter where there's a large wood table where they can design arrangements and a small office tucked in the corner.

"Start looking," he orders his men. "Tear this place apart."

I watch them start knocking things over, searching and destroying anything they come into contact with and I feel a prick of annoyance. I imagine she works hard to keep this business up and running and these idiots are demolishing it.

When Angelo starts dumping drawers in the office, I slowly start to back away, toward the front door. They're so busy dismantling everything in sight that I know now is my chance. I spin and make a run for it.

I shove a shoulder into the front door and my feet hit the pavement. I don't bother looking back, just take off across the parking lot, headed toward the street. It's not the busiest road, but several cars pass. There's a gas station across the street and that's where I'm headed.

When I reach the safety of the gas pumps, I turn around, breathing heavily. But, no one follows me. Maybe Angelo doesn't care about me anymore. All he wants are the diamonds and I gave him the information he needs. I walk into the small building where you pay and lift my bound hands.

"Got any scissors?" I ask.

The attendant's eyes widen and, a moment later, he cuts through the zip ties around my wrists.

"You okay?" he asks.

"Yeah. Can I use your phone?" The moment the words leave my mouth, I see a minivan pull into the parking lot across the street. I walk over to the window and squint. The driver's side door opens and a woman around 60 gets out. *Oh, shit.* It has to be Marina Lopez and she's about to walk into Angelo Savini on the rampage.

*What do I do?* She has no idea what's going on and what if they hurt her? I just told Angelo that she's the only one who knows where the diamonds are hidden.

I can't let them hurt her, I think, and run back outside. I hustle back across the street, but she's already stepping into the shop. *Dammit.*

I hurry over and skid to a halt in the entrance. Angelo looks up, his black eyes bright. "Decided to rejoin us, Harlow?" He has a gun trained on Marina and my gut twists.

Marina's brown eyes move over to me. "You're Robert's daughter," she says and gives me a warm smile.

I nod. I know nothing about this woman and I should be inclined to dislike her. But, I don't. There's something kind in her eyes. I know I can't leave her here with these assholes.

"Marina was just about to tell us where the diamonds are hidden," Angelo says.

But, she shakes her head and her stylish, dark bob swishes along her chin. "Robert told me you'd be coming, Mr. Savini, but I have no intention of telling you where I hid the diamonds. You may rot first," she adds in a feisty tone and I decide I really like this lady.

A thunderous look crosses Angelo's face and he stalks over to Marina and yanks her arm up behind her back. When she cries out, I run over. "Leave her alone," I say and grab onto his arm. He yanks free from my grip and backhands me across the face so hard that I spin and fall, my knees scraping across the floor.

I glare up at him and touch my split lip. *Bastard.*

"You misunderstand me, Marina. I'm not asking you," he says and digs his gun into her temple.

"I will never betray Robert," she says in a steady voice. "So, do what you must."

*Oh, God.* "Angelo," I say, trying to distract him. "She doesn't know."

"Fuck off, Harlow," he says, clearly not believing me.

I don't know why, but I can hear Bastian's voice: *Think fast, freckles.* "She used to know, but the cache was moved."

"What the hell are you talking about?" he asks and finally looks my way.

"When I visited my Dad, he asked me to move them. So, I did."

"You're telling me, you've known this whole time where the

diamonds are?" His eyes blaze with fury, but I don't care. I will not let him scare me.

"That's right. And, if you want them, you're going to have to let her go. She has nothing to do with it anymore."

Angelo makes a frustrated sound and looks from me back to Marina. "One of you knows and the other is a liar. Guess I'll just have to torture you both til I get the answer. Tie them up," he tells his men and lowers his gun.

I take a step back, reach behind me and my fingers wrap around a potted plant. The moment the first thug reaches me, I lift the pot and smash it against the side of his face. He falls to his knees with a grunt amidst a pile of dirt and ceramic shards.

I drop down and crawl down an aisle full of tall, potted palms. There aren't a lot of places to hide or go, but I keep moving away and search for something to use as a weapon. Up ahead, I see a small table with spools of ribbon and exactly what I'm looking for-- a nice, sharp pair of scissors.

Snagging the scissors, I continue forward, staying low and out of sight. At the end of the aisle, I see a red emergency exit sign and I start moving faster. Then, out of nowhere, a hand curls around my ankle and yanks me back. I scream and someone flips me around. Angelo drops down, straddling my middle, and I slash out with the scissors. I manage to slice his arm before he grabs my wrist and squeezes so hard that I drop my weapon with a cry. My wrist feels crushed.

"Bitch," he hisses and glances down at his torn, bloody sleeve. Then, he pins my hands against the floor and lowers his face to within an inch of mine. "If you think you can cut me and get away with it, you're mistaken." His black eyes move over me and I struggle not to cringe. "I'm going to enjoy breaking you. In every way possible."

I turn my head, refusing to look at him, and try to break free, but he's too heavy. "Get off me," I say between gritted teeth and twist beneath him.

"Oh, I'm gonna get off alright, Harlow. Especially when you're sucking me dry." He presses his thin lips against my neck and I freeze. Then, he bites the sensitive skin there hard and I give a yelp.

All of a sudden, I hear a commotion from the front of the store and someone yells, "Smoke grenade!"

There's a loud hissing noise and I see smoke begin to drift down the aisle toward us. Angelo glances over his shoulder and swears.

*Bastian,* I think. It must be the P.S. team. I hear some grunts, fighting and swearing from the front of the store and the sound of my guys beating up Angelo's goons is music to my ears.

Angelo heaves his weight off me, snags my wrist and yanks me toward the emergency exit. As we slam through the door, I scream Bastian's name.

Outside, we find ourselves in an alley behind the shop. I try to twist out of Angelo's grip, but he's too strong. So, I kick out and slam my heel against his shin. He cries out, lets me go and I take off.

My legs pump, hard and fast, my gaze on the end of the alley where I plan to hurl myself around the corner and circle back to the parking lot.

When a bullet whizzes past my head, I stop short and spin around.

"Take one more step and you're dead," Angelo warns me, slowly closing the distance between us, gun aimed at me.

*Fuck.*

"Let her go," a deep voice says.

I turn and see Bastian move into the alley. He's so close and I've never been so happy to see anyone in my life. All I want to do is throw myself into his arms and cover his face with kisses. But, I don't dare move. Angelo has his gun trained on me and I have no doubt in my mind that he will shoot me.

Standing between the two of them, my mind whirls. I'm much closer to Bastian, and can almost reach out and touch him. My gaze drops and I see the knife in his hand, but what good is that against a lunatic with a gun?

And, Angelo is closing in on us.

"I have your money," Bastian says and steps closer. He tosses the knife aside and slowly reaches into a pocket and removes a wad of cash. All the while moving closer to me. "Ten grand. All here. Take it and leave."

Then, he's at my side and I feel a wave of relief even though we aren't safe yet. But, knowing he's here, standing beside me, renews my strength and determination to defeat Angelo Savini once and for all.

"Piss on your money," Angelo says, also moving in, fearless because Bastian has no weapon now. "I want the diamonds."

"I don't know where they are," I say. "I lied. So, keeping me won't get you anything."

A rage like I've never seen before fills Angelo's eyes and without warning, he lifts the gun and starts shooting. Bastian slams into me and we go down hard. Covering me with his big body, pressing me into the concrete, Bastian tries to protect me from Angelo and my heart thumps madly.

*Oh, God, I don't want to die.* Not here in this dirty back alley when I'm so close to finding happiness with this man. There is so much that I want to tell him, so many things he needs to know. And, first and foremost, I'm going to tell him how very much I love him.

When I feel Bastian's body jerk above me then begin to slide off me and down to the ground, my heart stops, and a cold terror grips me.

*No, no, no.*

I scramble out from beneath him and, from the corner of my eye, I see Ryker sneak up behind Angelo and bring him down with the butt of his pistol.

I roll Bastian over onto his back and he groans in pain. My gaze dips and I see blood soaking through his t-shirt. "Nooo," I cry. "Bastian, look at me." I cup his face, forcing him to focus on me. "You're going to be okay. You have to be."

But, his beautiful hazel eyes glaze over and there's so much blood. I don't know what to do so I shove my hands against the wound, trying to staunch the waterfall of blood. Panic hits me, clamping me down in its jaws, and I look up through tear-filled eyes to see Jax race out the emergency exit.

"Jax!" I scream.

Jax drops to his knees beside me, rips Bastian's shirt apart and examines the gunshot wound.

"Why is there so much blood?" I ask.

"Probably nicked an artery. *Fuck*," Jax swears. He reaches beneath Bastian's shoulder and probes the wound and a cry rips from Bastian's throat. "There's an exit hole." I think I hear what sounds like a bit of relief in his voice.

"That's good, right?" I ask.

"Yeah, but we need to call 911."

As Jax makes the call, I take Bastian's face in my hands again and feel him wrap his fingers around my wrist in a loose grip. His eyes are bright with pain, a little unfocused, and he grimaces. "Help will be here soon," I tell him. "You just hang in there, okay?"

His mouth edges up slightly as he looks up at me.

"What?" I ask.

"Reminds me how we met, freckles..." His grip loosens, falls away. Then, his hazel eyes glaze over and shut.

My heart shatters and I grab his hand, lift his battered knuckles up and press my lips against them, along each number tattooed there representing the dates his parents and sister died. *God, please don't let this be the day Bastian dies.* My heart constricts and I feel Jax lay a hand on my shoulder. "Please, be okay. *Please*," I whisper.

"Help will be here soon," he says.

I glance up and see Ryker has Angelo on his knees, hands zip tied. I'm sure Griff has the other two subdued and is keeping watch inside the shop.

I glare at Angelo and want nothing more than to stomp over there, pick up his gun and shoot him. Give him a taste of his own medicine.

Yeah, I have no problem with revenge when it's deserved.

It doesn't take long for an ambulance to arrive and I watch closely as they start to work on Bastian and exchange a few words with Jax. The police pull up a minute later and Ryker hands Angelo over. But, the police have a lot of questions.

After the ambulance pulls away, I fall into Jax's arms and I do something I haven't done in years. I sob my eyes out. He strokes my hair back, exchanging looks with Griff and Ryker who must think I'm nothing but a weepy female.

"He's gonna be okay, Harlow," Griff says and wanders up next to us. He lays a hand on my shoulder and I look up into his bright blue eyes.

"What if he's not?"

"They said the bullet went straight through," Jax tells me again. Probably for the tenth time, but I can't seem to wrap my head around everything that just happened. Worry is shredding my insides.

Ryker moves up on my other side and squeezes my shoulder. "Bastian's tough. Hell, we've all been shot. Now he's a part of the club."

I swipe my tears away and look from Ryker to Griff to Jax, so grateful for these three alpha men who are trying their best to make me feel better. They're like three more brothers and I love them to pieces.

"After we finish up with the police, I'll drive us over to the hospital, okay?" Jax says.

"Okay. Where's Angelo?" I ask, eyes darting to the shop.

The guys shift, exchange more conspiratorial looks. "Trust me when I say Angelo Savini won't ever bother you or my brother again," Jax says.

"Don't worry, ShadowWalker, we took care of it," Griff assures me.

"The only place Angelo is going is back to prison-- with a few broken bones-- for a very long time," Ryker adds.

With a nod, I sniff and look up to see Marina standing in the doorway. "Can we talk?" she asks.

The guys look to me, brows raised, and I nod. "I'll be okay," I tell them. As they move away, I head back into the flower shop.

"I'm sorry about your man," she says and hands me a tissue.

*My man.* "Thank you," I say and wipe my nose. I must look like an absolute wreck.

Marina looks around at all the destruction that Angelo and his goons caused, but she doesn't seem overly upset. "I'm just happy we got to meet," she says. "Despite the circumstances. Your Dad speaks very highly of you."

*What?* I did not expect to hear that. "He does?"

"Oh, yes. He brags about how smart you are-- a computer genius, he says."

Her revelation surprises me. I never thought my Dad gave two shits about me, to be honest. "So, you and my Dad..."

"Despite all of his flaws, and we both know he has quite a few, I love him dearly."

*Hmm.* Maybe Marina and I have some things in common, I realize.

"He loves you, too," she says.

I let out a sound of disbelief. "He sure has a funny way of showing it."

"He's made a lot of mistakes. But, if you can find it in your heart to forgive him, I don't believe he will ever let you down again."

Her words are nice, but I'm not naive enough to believe them.

With a small smile, Marina walks over to one of the few plants that Angelo and his men didn't smash. It's a bundle of bamboo stalks in a vase tied with a red ribbon. She hands it to me. "It will bring you good luck and good fortune."

I take the plant and study the pretty stones that hold its roots in place. I'm not sure what to say, but despite all of my turbulent feelings toward my father, I can't help but like Marina Lopez. Maybe she's a good influence on him and, when he gets out of prison, she can help keep him on the straight and narrow path.

I suppose stranger things have happened.

"Bob and I wish you and Bastian every happiness and plenty of good fortune." There's a twinkle in her eye as she hands me the bamboo.

"Harlow," Jax calls and sticks his dark head in the doorway. "Ready to go to the hospital?"

I look up and nod. "Be right there." I turn back to Marina. "Thank you," I say. "And, it was nice meeting you, too."

As I walk away, Marina tells me one more thing. "Don't forget-- your father loves you, Harlow. Sometimes things aren't always what they seem."

With her words echoing in my head, I go outside.

# 20

# BASTIAN

After two days in the hospital, the doctor clears me. And, the entire time, Harlow remains by my side. No one has ever stayed by me like that, night and day. She even fed me jello.

"It's the least I can do," she had said. "After all, you did take a bullet for me."

No one ever fed me jello before and Harlow did in the sexiest way possible. It's something I won't forget any time soon.

They bandaged my shoulder up pretty good and it's hard to move around so Harlow drives us back to Jax's apartment which now is pretty much my place since he's living with Easton. I finally met my brother's new wife the other day when she and Jax came to visit. And, damn, he's a lucky man.

*So, am I,* I think, and look over at Harlow.

Honestly, I'm not sure how I survived so long without her. She's brought so much to my life in such a short amount of time. She's *everything.*

In the hospital, I decided I'm getting a tattoo for her-- four interlocking circles and a fifth one that overlays and connects the rest. The symbol for everything. Who knows? Maybe I'll be a bad influence on her and she will get one, too.

When we get back to the apartment, Harlow fusses over me. She helps me change into my pajama bottoms, slip into bed and then fluffs the pillows behind my head. I'm not going to lie. I like it.

"You'd make a good nurse," I say as she sits down on the bed beside me.

"Only to you," she says. "I can't imagine having strangers as patients. It takes a special kind of person to do that."

"You're about as special as they get," I say and she gives me a little half-smile.

"When did you get so mushy?" she asks.

For a long moment I don't say anything. But, now is the perfect time to tell her how I feel. *Do it, Bastian. For once in your life, be honest with yourself.*

I reach out and trail a finger over the back of her hand. "I think it happened when I fell in love with you."

"Bastian..." Something sparks in the depths of her blue-gray eyes and she laces her fingers through mine.

"I know I'm a handful, but I think we're really good together. I've been selfish for a really long time and I'm so sick of being a fuck-up. I'm ready to finally take on some responsibility. To not feel so damn useless anymore." I let out an unsteady breath and press a hand to my bandage. My heart is beating hard, so fast that I feel like I'm going to have a heart attack if Harlow doesn't say something soon.

But, I don't even give her a chance. I just keep spewing words that I hope make sense as they come tumbling out. "And, I know you said I remind you of your Dad and that scares you. But, I see what a toll your relationship with him takes on you. And, I don't ever want to inflict that kind of pain on you. I promise, Harlow."

"You don't scare me, Bastian," she says and moves her fingers through mine. "And, I trust you..." As her voice trails off, anxiety floods my stomach. I feel like a *but* is coming.

Her steel blue eyes meet mine. "But..."

*Fuck. Here it comes.*

She doesn't love me.

"But, I hope you understand that after all we've been through and everything you just said-- you are never getting rid of me. Because I love you, Sebastian. So, so much."

Relief floods through me and I yank her forward against my chest. I ignore the pain that shoots through my shoulder and I capture her mouth in a desperate kiss.

"Your wound," she says and tries to pull back.

But, I don't let go. "Fuck it. Just keep your mouth moving on mine." Harlow kisses me again, but she's extremely careful not to lean too hard against me. "I'm not going to break," I tell her and reach down, sliding my hand down the front of her leggings.

"Bastian," she gasps. "We can't."

But, I am not taking no for an answer. This amazing woman just said she loves me and now I plan to make love to her. Hot and slow. "We can and we are going to right now. Just be gentle with me," I say and nip her earlobe as my fingers circle and dip and tease inside her panties.

When her breath hitches and her hips buck against my hand, I know I have her right where I want her. "Come for me," I whisper and slide a finger inside her wet warmth. Harlow drops her head, breathing hard, that gorgeous dark hair spilling down my bare chest and filling my nose with the scent of sweet strawberries. A moment later, she cries out.

"Help me get these off," I say, urgently tugging at my pajama bottoms, so hungry with desire that my hands shake. We yank them down part way, get Harlow's off all the way and then she carefully moves over me, dropping a knee on either side of me. I grip her hips and she lifts up over my swollen cock, positioning herself above the moist tip.

*Heaven.*

"No more condoms," she whispers and begins to slide down my thick, pulsating shaft. "I got a contraceptive implant while we were at the hospital."

I groan as she sinks all the way down. "I get the feeling you're going to be a bad influence."

"On you? Ha!"

As Harlow begins to rock her hips, establishing a rhythm, grinding downward, I lean back into the pile of pillows and savor the ride and the view. She tosses her head back, eyes closed, lips parted and I love the way she moves.

I slide my hand over the curve of her hip and down between us, circling her clit, pressing, finding exactly what she likes when she lets out a low, throaty moan. "You feel so good," I say, unable to drag my eyes away as she comes.

As the waves of pleasure ripple through her body, she clenches around me and I rear up and feel my own release hit, hot and sweet. My hips surge up and when I empty into her body with a climax that steals my breath away, it's pure ecstasy.

I sink into the pillows, pulling her with me, wrapping my arms around her. She looks up, traces a finger along the edge of the big, white bandage. "How's your shoulder?" she asks.

"I'm doped up on painkillers, sweetheart. So, pretty good," I say with a smirk. I run a hand through her hair. "You know, for the first time in my life, I feel damn lucky."

Harlow lifts her head and kisses me so slowly and with so much love that I feel longing for her rise up within me all over again. "Maybe it's the bamboo," she teases and we both glance over at the green stalks on my dresser.

"No," I say and pull her down against me, placing a kiss along her hairline. "It's all you, freckles."

# EPILOGUE

## HARLOW

Eventually, I move over and give Bastian more room to sleep. I know he said he was feeling fine, but he needs to rest. For a moment, I watch his steady, even breathing. Then, I take a look at his bandage. When I'm sure he's fine, I slide out of bed.

I walk over to the dresser, slide a drawer open and pull out one of his t-shirts to sleep in. After I drop it over my head, my gaze lands on the bamboo in the vase.

*Sometimes things aren't always what they seem.*

Marina's words reverberate through my head as I lean forward and study the pretty rocks at the bottom of the vase. They look like pieces of quartz pebbles or pale colored glass.

*It couldn't be.*

Thoughts swirl through my head as I grab the vase and head toward the living room. I flip a light on and grab my laptop. Then, I pull up a search engine and type in "rough uncut diamonds." When I read the description of what uncut diamonds look like, my mouth drops. All this time, I thought we were talking about brilliant, sparkling diamonds like you see in a jewelry store.

A moment later, I dump the water down the kitchen sink and spill the stones out on a plate. I carry the plate back to the couch and sit.

"Hey."

I look up and see Bastian. "What're you doing out of bed?" I ask.

"Had to go to the bathroom, if that's okay."

I motion for him to come over. "Well, now that you're up, tell me what you think about this."

He ambles over, still looking sleepy and hair sticking up all over the place. He sits on the couch beside me, eyeing the plate. I turn my laptop screen filled with images of uncut diamonds in his direction. "What is this?" he asks and scratches his chest.

"I think the pebbles with the bamboo aren't pebbles at all."

His hazel eyes widen. "Oh, shit."

"When Marina gave me the vase, she told me that she and my Dad wished us every happiness and plenty of good fortune. I think they gave us his share of the diamonds."

"Unbelievable." He picks up one of the stones and studies it. "Who would ever guess this was a diamond?"

"I mean, I don't know for sure. But, my gut tells me yes."

"Guess we can have someone check them out," he says and sets the stone back on the plate.

I nod and stand up. "Back to bed, Mr. Wilder. You need your rest." He smiles sleepily and I take his hand, guiding him back to the bedroom. Back into my arms.

The next day, Bastian and I take the stones over to a diamond expert and after a quick examination, he assures us the gems are real. He estimates they're worth around $5 million and when he starts asking questions, we provide vague answers and skip out fast.

Back in the car, I look over at Bastian, my conscience roiling. He knows what I'm about to say and he smiles. "Whatever you want to do, I support you."

I let out a breath and look down at the velvet bag in my hands. "These belong to a Saudi Arabian prince not me."

"I'm pretty sure he'd want them back, too."

"Yeah. Here's the thing, though. The gemologist said these were worth $5 million." Bastian nods. "My Dad stole $20 million in diamonds. Palmer took his half, but that still leaves another $5 million unaccounted for."

"You think Marina has them?"

I let out a laugh. "Probably. Who the hell knows where, but, yeah, I think there's definitely another $5 million somewhere."

"Crazy."

"I'm going to do some digging. See what I can find out about this prince. If there's anything shady about how he makes his money, I'm not giving these back. But, if he's a good guy then I'll reach out to him. That sound okay?"

"You're a good person," he says and reaches for my hand. "You guided me back to the light and away from the dark. No one ever did that for me before."

"I don't know about that, but I'll always be here to pull you back."

"I love you, Harlow Vaughn," he says, green-gold eyes so full of emotion that I feel my chest tighten.

"More than diamonds?" I ask.

Bastian leans in and captures my mouth in a soul-rending kiss. "More than strawberries," he whispers and taps my nose.

Later that evening, Easton and Jax invite everyone up to their place in the Hollywood Hills. Jax is all moved in and Bastian has officially taken over his old apartment. It's nice because it's so close to me, but at the same time, I'm rarely at my place anymore. In fact, we're talking about moving in together soon.

It's funny because I never used to leave my apartment. I was like a hermit, locked up in my dark office, gaze glued on multiple monitors, nose buried on the Dark Web. But, now I've learned there are more important things than work. Like Bastian and my family at Platinum Security.

And, Marina and, dare I say, my Dad. After a long talk with Bastian, and a bit of convincing, I've decided to give my Dad another chance and try to mend our relationship. Even if it doesn't work out, the fact that I forgive him has lifted a huge weight off my heart. I'm not sure what the future will bring, but I'm visiting him this weekend, along with Bastian and Marina.

I have high hopes.

I also finally got a chance to talk to my older brothers and fill them in on everything that's been happening. Dane is still busy teaching up at the sniper school and Rafe, as usual, is vague about where he is and what he's doing. It seems like everything he does is classified. But, when I tell him about the diamonds and that I want to possibly give them back to the Saudi Arabian prince, he tells me to wait until he does a background check.

Turns out the prince likes to sell weapons to terrorists. So, I'll be keeping the diamonds.

I'm sure I can find a better way to put them to good use and help others in the process. Marina had mentioned an organization that visits the prison and that helped my Dad. It's called Paws For Life and matches an inmate with a rescue dog. Over the course of 12 weeks, the prisoners partner with a dog to teach basic commands, behavior and socialization to help prepare them for adoption.

Marina tells me a lot of participants in the program have even had their sentences commuted.

I'm thinking they could use a sizable, anonymous donation.

As we pull up Mr. and Mrs. Wilder's circular driveway, I see the house is lit up like a Christmas tree, literally, with endless strands of lights outside along the house and strung in all the nearby trees. After all, Christmas is only a week away and it looks like Easton had an entire crew here to help decorate.

It looks warm and welcoming and it makes me smile. Easton told me her huge mansion used to feel cold and empty until Jax and the rest of us came into her life. Now, as Bastian and I walk through the front door, holding hands, it's bright with light, laughter and love.

And, so many Christmas decorations that I don't know where to look first.

Lexi swoops in and gives me a hug and Avery and Easton are close behind. I can't help but laugh at her ugly Christmas sweater. "Wait til you see Griff's," she says with a chuckle. "It's godawful."

The girls pull me away from Bastian and I give him a helpless shrug. We sit in front of a roaring fire and, on the edge of their seats, they demand details about me and Bastian and all the excitement and drama that went down.

It's also pretty adorable to see two handmade stockings hanging from the mantle that say Jax on one and Easton on the other.

I fill them in, answer their questions and I'm so grateful to be able to call these amazing women my friends. I love them to death and know they have my back just like I have theirs.

Not far away, Bastian talks with Jax, Griff and Ryker. At one point, he glances up, a candy cane hanging from his mouth like a cigarette, and gives me a flirty nod and wink. He'll always be a bad boy, I think, and I love it.

I never thought it would be possible to love a man as much as I love Sebastian Wilder. Yet, here I am, head over heels and enjoying every delicious minute of it.

Eventually, everyone winds up by the crackling fire in the arms of the person he or she loves and Bastian pulls me onto his lap. We all drink Easton's expensive champagne and pick from a scattering of dessert trays. I grab a chocolate-covered strawberry and feed it to Bastian. "Your favorite," I say and he takes a bite.

"Not nearly as sweet as you, freckles," he says and kisses me. My toes curl and he tastes like strawberries and champagne. Utterly yummy.

"We're glad you all made it over for an early Christmas celebration," Jax says, arms wrapped around Easton. "Although this one may have gone a little overboard decorating."

He nods his dark head to the 20-foot tall tree full of blinking lights and ornaments and we laugh. *Leave it to Easton,* I think, and chuckle.

A smile curves her bright red lips. "It's our first Christmas together. For all of us," she adds and he kisses the top of her head. "I wanted to make it memorable."

"I'll tell you what's memorable," Ryker says and nods at Griff. "That hideous sweater. Where the hell did you find that monstrosity?"

"You're just jealous, Flynn," Griff says and runs a proud hand over the ugly sweater. Lexi flicks a bell sewn onto the sweater and laughs.

Griff grabs her hand and twines his fingers through hers. They share a look and then make an announcement.

"We picked a date," Lexi says. "Everybody mark February 14 on your calendar."

"I'm marrying my redhead on Valentine's Day," Griff adds.

They share a kiss and aww's and a couple of low whistles fill the air.

"Should we tell them?" I hear Avery ask Ryker in a low voice. I look over and he nods, a large, protective hand sliding down over her stomach.

Ryker clears his throat and Avery leans back in his arms, gazing up at him with so much love and adoration that my eyes nearly tear up. "We're going to have a baby," he announces, his voice rough with emotion.

Congratulations fill the festive air and the guys slap Ryker on the back.

"You're going to make an amazing Dad," Griff says.

"Thanks. That means a lot," Ryker says. Then, Griff and Ryker do their little signature handshake where they slide palms, grip fingers and bump knuckles.

"Congratulations," Jax says and repeats the handshake with Ryker. He slants a glance at Bastian. "Gonna have to teach you the Platinum Security handshake. As you guys know, business is booming. Which is great, but that means we need more help. So, I decided to add a few new additions to the team...starting with Bastian." I can tell Jax is bursting with pride. And, so am I. "Bastian is coming onboard as an investigator and will act as our liaison with Detective Logan Sharpe over at LAPD."

"Welcome to the team," Ryker says.

I press a kiss to Bastian's cheek and more cheers fill the air.

"Hey, and you even have the war wounds. You'll fit right in," Griff teases. "How's the gunshot healing up, by the way?"

"Better than expected," Bastian says. "And, I've got quite the attentive nurse here to help take care of it."

They laugh.

"So, who else is joining our little dysfunctional family?" Griff asks.

"We also have Ryker's friend and former Navy SEAL Cole Drake starting next week."

"Nice," Griff says. "He helped me and Lexi a couple of months ago on her case. Back when you didn't like me very much, Red," he adds and tickles her side.

Lexi squeals, twisting in his arms. "Please. I liked you from the moment I laid eyes on your CIA dossier."

Griff playfully narrows his eyes at her and I pretend not to hear that since I was the one who sent his private dossier to Lexi. I don't feel bad, though, because look how it turned out.

"And," Jax says, "I just got a call from Ryker and Avery's contact in Columbia, Grayson Shaw, who will be here by the end of the month. He's former CIA and has some good contacts."

"Both good guys," Ryker says.

"You know, if it weren't for Gray, we never would've gotten together," Avery says.

"We definitely owe him," Ryker says and tightens his arms around Avery. "Maybe we should name our firstborn after him."

Avery just smiles and then pulls Ryker's head down and whispers something in his ear. He nods and they share a kiss.

As I look around our growing circle, I'm so happy and full of love, I could burst. Never in a million years would I have imagined that the anti-social loner who barely left her apartment last year would suddenly find herself with an incredible group of girlfriends, alpha male protectors who would fight to the death for me and the love of a lifetime who makes my heart trip every time I look at him.

It's been quite a journey for all of us. A lot of healing has taken place, demons overcome and past trauma and guilt healed. Deep down, I think everyone is a little broken. But, that's how the light gets in, right?

I lift my champagne glass and a moment later everyone else follows suit. "To the past six months and all the family, friends, light and love that it has brought each of us. I love you guys." A sheen of tears blurs my vision and Bastian drops his face and kisses my cheek.

"Cheers!" We all clink glasses and have no doubt that the future will bring endless love and good fortune.

* * *

Want to know if their HEA includes a proposal? Read the *Dark Secrets* Extended Epilogue to find out.

***

Want to read more about the irresistible alpha bad boys at Platinum Security? If you liked Harlow and Bastian's story, you'll love reading about Grayson and Charlotte's romantic suspense adventure in *Stars and Scars.*

# EXTENDED EPILOGUE

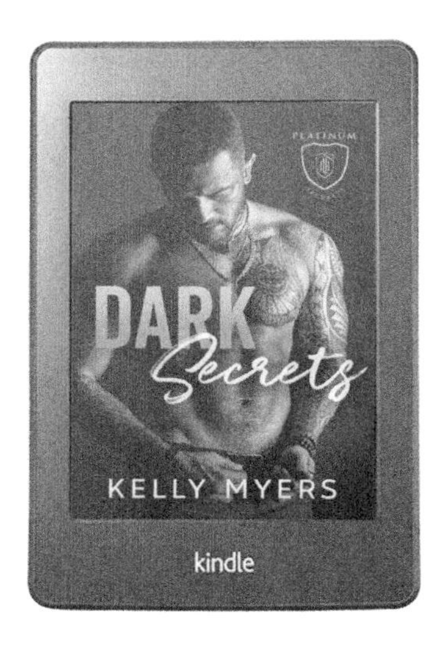


Want to know if their HEA includes a proposal?

Read the *Dark Secrets* Extended Epilogue to find out:

**Get Free Extended Epilogue**

# READ NEXT: STARS AND SCARS

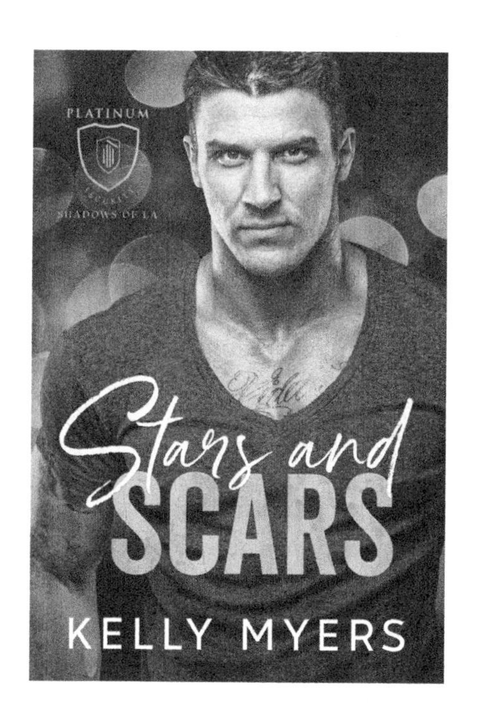


**He's haunted by his past, and she's fighting for her future.**

As a rising influencer in Los Angeles, Charlotte seems to have it all – the followers, the likes, the sponsors. But it's not all roses behind the filters. And when an online cult targets Charlotte with chilling threats, her picture-perfect world starts to crumble.

Her only hope? Grayson, an ex-CIA agent turned bodyguard from Platinum Security.

Grayson is everything Charlotte is not – secretive, intense, and deeply guarded. From the moment they meet, the attraction is undeniable, but so are their differences. He's all about control and stealth; she's about sharing every moment. Yet, with faceless enemies lurking at every turn, he's the only one she can trust.

As the threats escalate, so does the tension between them. Driven to hide off-grid together, Grayson sees beyond her carefully curated persona, and Charlotte glimpses the depths of the man behind the stoic facade. Their forced proximity reveals a passionate connection that cannot be ignored. But they also uncover a conspiracy of deception and betrayal.

Can their connection survive the deadly threats closing in on them, or will their deepest scars be their undoing?

## Chapter One: Charlotte

Most people shut off their alarm and shuffle into the bathroom to begin their daily grooming in private. I'm not most people.

With a jaw-crackingly huge yawn, I swing my legs over the side of the bed. The sun has yet to kiss the LA basin, and won't for a couple of hours yet. I've lived in Los Angeles my entire life, but I used to rise with the sun. Now, my day begins at 4:30 AM, just like every day.

I answer the call of nature and then hit play on my Megan Trainer wakeup playlist. Before I start filming content, I have to make myself somewhat presentable. I use a cold compress to take swelling down in my face, then pull my unruly black hair back into a tight bun.

Nobody on the internet can smell my breath, but I go ahead and brush my teeth anyway. The minty tingle helps me feel more like a human. After that I tie a knot at the waist of my tank top to make it sleek and tight. Only when I'm done with all of my preparations do I turn on the ring light and begin filming.

"Hello beautiful people of Charlottesville! It's a little past 4:30, so my brain's still a little foggy. That's why I'm glad that Globaline's new cosmetics line is so easy to use. I'm going to start with a basic foundation..."

I smooth the beige powder over my cheeks, then use a brush to blend it.

"As you can see, those blemishes are going bye-bye. I plan on getting more sun this summer, so I'll have to update my shade. But don't worry, Globaline makes it easy with their skin-tone matching app."

As I finish my pre-workout skincare routine, I glance at the checklist on the pink sticky note hanging from my mirror. I have to make sure I hit all of my endorsements for the day. Thank goodness most of my 2.3 million followers understand the hustle. Sponsored endorsements saved my family.

Everybody wants to be an influencer. Money for nothing! Never have to work a day in your life! That's not exactly true. Still, I feel incredibly lucky that it's worked out for me, so far.

"Ok, that's it for now, see you next time in Charlottesville!"

After my skincare routine, it's time for a workout. I grab my strawberry lemonade energy drink and head down the hall, flanked by a view of the pre-dawn cityscape. I wonder how many other points of light belong to people starting their work day, just like me.

At the end of the hall, I hang a left and enter my home gym. Thanks to product placement deals, I have all of the latest, highest tech equipment. My exercise bike has more computing power than the rocket ship the first astronauts took to the moon. My scale will tell me everything from my weight to my ambient skin temperature and cholesterol levels.

The fitness regime is crucial. Everyone knows the internet is without mercy or pity. But even more than that, it helps me stay healthy, and my followers say it helps them too.

I flip on the lights, check my image on the monitor, and mount the elliptical machine. Once I start recording, my smile comes back like magic.

"Hey, what up my peeps? It's exercise time in Charlottesville. Thanks to my XFitt 2500 elliptical machine, I don't have to sacrifice comfort for results. The gyroscopic balancing and extra-responsive controls mean I'm always in charge of my workout."

I set the elliptical to about seventy percent of my max output. I still need to be able to talk, after all.

"You can easily adjust the settings with a flick of a switch, or by voice, like this: Xfitt, increase angle by 4 percent."

The arms adjust with a mechanical whirr and I beam at the camera.

"It really is that easy. Oh, and I almost forgot, I want to say a huge thank you to everyone who voted for me in the LA's Points of Brightness awards. You're the best! I'm super stoked to be a recipient for my work with the UCLA Mattel Children's Hospital. Thanks so much for your support!"

A sheen of sweat glistens on my forehead, but it's not creating too much of a glare. I check my filters and make sure everything looks good. Unlike my skincare routine, I'm livestreaming the workout so everything has to be perfect.

So far, so good. I roll through a couple more endorsements, then find I have about ten minutes of blank space to fill. The hearts and likes keep on coming as I switch gears to something more personal.

"Now I'd like to shout out to my favorite people in the world... Hey Mom and Dad! I see you're watching, which I love, but I need you to sign off for a few minutes. I have a surprise to share with you later." I wait until my parents are offline and then continue in a stage whisper.

"So, my parent's thirtieth wedding anniversary is coming up, and I want to do something special for them. Since y'all have such great ideas, I'd love to hear what you think. I've created a poll you can link to from my social pages. Thanks fam!"

I finish my workout, and post my results for my followers to see. Someone points out that I completed my steps in record time today. I thank them and shut off the cameras for a while.

As soon as I stop filming, my smile fades and I droop between the armrests of the elliptical machine. I don't even feel all that tired, not physically, but being 'on stage' all the time can be exhausting. Sometimes, I wish I had a normal job.

But then I wouldn't get to be part of my followers' amazing stories. And I mean their real stories, not the social sharing feature. Like Jenny, who used my dating profile advice to get her first online date after divorce. Or Margot, who gained the confidence from my makeup and hair tutorials to land her dream job. Then there's Sarah, who feels like she has her body back post-pregnancy, partly thanks to my workout routine.

I'm about to step in the shower when my phone rings. I check the screen and smile when I see it's my mom. Wrapping myself up in a fluffy robe, I sit on the edge of the tub.

"Hey mama, what's up?"

"Hi honey, I just wanted to see how you're doing."

"I'm great, just about to wash off my workout sweat and head out to meet the team. How are you?"

"We're doing just fine–"

Apparently I'm on speaker, because my dad cuts in. "Ask her about the surprise!"

Mom makes a 'tsk' sound and I chuckle as I picture her pinching Dad's arm.

"As you like to say, Dad, patience is a virtue. Too bad this virtue's still on backorder."

I can practically hear my dad wink as he says, "that's my girl."

Mom clears her throat and I think I know what's coming next.

"Charlotte, you've been working so hard lately. Are you taking some time for yourself? Making plans with friends?"

Just as I suspected. "I spend time with my friends every day, all day. That's the great thing about my job."

My mom's frown is audible through the phone. "Well, I just want you to be able to really live your life. You know, take a break, unplug. I worry about you."

If she only knew about the haters and idle threats, like the one I got last week. She would insist I quit social media immediately. Which is why I don't tell her about them.

"Don't worry Mom, once I land this big sponsor today, I'll be able to relax a bit."

I think Mom wants to say more, but instead she says, "Ok honey, sounds good. Well we better get to work."

We end with a chorus of 'I love yous,' and I set the phone down with a sigh.

All the time and effort I spend to support my parents, and they still have to work. Even worse, I hardly get to spend any time with them. But hopefully that's going to change soon.

Not that I'm complaining. My parents worked two, sometimes three jobs at a time to make sure I got enough to eat and could attend a decent school. I have no problem paying them back in kind.

And besides, my life is great. I get to hang out with celebrities, try the latest brands and fashions for free–Heck, they pay me to try them most of the time–and don't have to worry too much about money.

True, it would be nice if I had a little more time to enjoy it. And maybe someone special to enjoy it with. But even if I had the time, dating in LA is hard. A lot of men can masquerade under a veil of charm that falls away the second they get comfortable with you. So I stick with what works, for now.

The sun is a red line on the horizon when I finish my shower and slip into leggings and an oversize top. My wardrobe team is due to meet me at the PCC flea market in an hour. It's going to be a big day filming content and I have to be at my best.

I stop and pose on the hood of my red Lexus. I'm supposed to create at least three endorsement social media posts about the car every week. In exchange, I get to keep on leasing it, and they even foot the bill for my fuel. In LA, where you have to drive everywhere, this is huge.

Once I've posted about the car, I get behind the wheel and drive to the flea market. By the time I spot my team's big, green van in the parking lot, the sun is well into the azure sky. I slip on a pair of shades before locking the Lexus and joining my team.

"Good morning, everyone. Leslie, is that coffee for me?"

"Yes ma'am, here you go."

"Thanks Leslie, you're a lifesaver."

I take the coffee from Leslie's wizened grip. She's around seventy and still has the magic touch when it comes to styling hair. Behind her, my make up artist Ramone fans herself with a folded up event program. Steve, my pink-shirted, impeccably mustachioed camera man, gives me a wave.

"How's Whiskers doing?" I ask Steve.

"She's doing much better now, and getting used to having no claws. She's even making her happy cat noises again. I recorded a few that are gonna make great sound effects."

I chuckle. "What would I do without you?"

"You would live a sad, boring life," Steve says with a wink.

My team came together more or less organically. It all started with Leslie, the lady who lived across the hall from me in my old apartment, offering to do my hair.

She did such a good job, and we got along so well, we continued to collaborate. Then she mentioned that her nephew Stephen was looking for work, and one thing led to another.

We've been together for almost four and a half years now. Having people I can rely on is important to me, enough that I give them all a percentage of my earnings. After all, Charlottesville isn't just me, it's an entire brand and they have been such a big part of it.

Steve looks up from his phone. "It's looking good today, no chance of rain."

Greg, his partner and my stylist, rolls his eyes. "You can't trust the internet weather report. My knee tells me it's going to rain."

"Well, hopefully it won't happen until we're done for the day," Steve counters.

Greg peers at me and purses his lips. "I'm thinking that you should be in denim today, girl. Something that goes with the, shall we say rustic nature of flea marketing."

Steve snorts. "As long as she looks cute, and not like she hails from a place where people go to the family reunion to hook up."

I slap him on the arm. "Be nice, Steve. We all have to be at our best to snag Etsy."

We've been after the e-commerce giant for months, and they finally agreed to a kind of tryout. If I get enough views at the flea market today, they'll consider sponsoring me. With Etsy backing my channel, I would be able to give my parents the long overdue gift of retirement.

I try on a couple different outfits before settling on a pair of cutoff shorts and a sleeveless Tee with the Pasadena City College logo emblazoned on the front. The idea is to look approachable and flea market apropos while still being fashion forward. When I see myself on the monitor, I start losing confidence.

"This is a lot more leg than I'm used to showing. Do my undies show when I bend over?"

I do a test bend while Leslie peers intently.

"Nah, you're good. The shorts are short, but they don't ride up."

I look around to get the consensus from the rest of my team. Everyone seems to think I look good enough to film. I let my team doll me up to look camera-ready and then prepare to start streaming. Steve counts down.

"Ok we're live in 5-4-"

I tug on my shorts and bite my lip. Even after all this time I still get nervous going live, especially when I'm out in the world. At home, I'm in complete control. Out in public, anything can happen. I take a deep breath and picture my parents smiling faces.

Steve switches to fingers to show we're live in 3-2-1.

"Hey, Charlottesville peeps, I'm at the World Famous PCC Flea Market. I'm here trying to nail down some great deals. Remember my old side table? Well, out with the old, in with the new."

I pick up the side table and give it a toss off camera. Steve times the whistling noise just right, as well as the yowl implying I struck a cat. Steve wasn't lying about getting some great sounds from Whiskers.

I lead the way down the flea market's main walkway. The sight of a camera induces one of two reactions in the vendors. Either they light up and get cheery about the free advertising…or they roll their eyes and prepare to endure another 'influencer.' I try to keep myself as unoffensive as possible, and avoid the vendors who look like they would rather not deal with me.

Live Streaming is not for the faint of heart. You have to keep up a steady flow of narration while looking for the next thing to talk about. Plus, you have to make sure you don't develop a snot bubble or fall on your face. The first time I went live was a complete disaster. But now I actually enjoy it, once I get over the initial nerves.

I stop in a little stall that has some mid-century modern furnishings. The proprietor is a sixtyish man with a long gray beard. When he turns out to be one of my followers, I'm downright ecstatic.

I pose with a few different end tables he has, and my followers reply with hearts or thumbs down emojis. I wind up picking the table with medium popularity.

He tries to give me a discount, but I wind up overpaying out of guilt. It's bad optics to be one of those people who is always trying to work the discount or freebie angle.

I walk around the flea market for half an hour, livestreaming the whole time. The numbers aren't as good as I'm used to, but it's a lovely Saturday morning and I know a lot of my followers will play the video on their own time.

"All right, everyone. Now I'm going to–"

My screen goes dark. Frowning, I tap on the screen and see that my phone is still on. It's the feed that's been interrupted.

"Hey, Leslie, can I see your phone? My stream has gone dark."

A bleeding eye symbol flashes over the screen, and then a sinister, electronically distorted voice speaks.

"We are the Aegis Order. We have usurped this insipid video to deliver a warning. Our social-media driven culture has led to a death of intellectualism and a rise in rampant consumerism."

"Well sonofabitch. Is this some kinda joke?" Leslie says, showing me her phone. "I've got the same thing on mine."

Steve comes over and peers over her shoulder. His face goes pale.

"It's not a joke! I've heard about these people, some kind of hacktivist group."

"Like Anonymous?" I ask.

"Way worse than Anonymous. Anonymous just leaks data. The Order makes threats."

"Why are they cutting into my feed, though? Shouldn't they be screwing with a Kardashian or something?"

I start to feel panicky. This is going to ruin my chances with Etsy.

The video switches to scenes of people at shopping malls, online purchasing sites, and stacks of money being counted.

"Social Media Influencers are destroying the very fabric of our society. People without talent or creativity are making ludicrous amounts of money and winning awards they don't deserve."

The video cuts to a headline with my picture next to the Points of Brightness award.

"We have chosen Charlotte Gilroy, AKA CharlottesVille4-Ever, to be an example to others. If Charlotte does not stop posting content online, there will be consequences."

"Wait a minute," I say, gripping my phone with white knuckle intensity. "These are the same guys who sent me that creepy direct message last week. They told me to stop posting or face consequences, and then there was a skull and crossbones emoji..."

Leslie gasps. "Did you call the police?"

"No."

"Why the Hell not?"

I sigh. "Leslie, I get at least a half dozen death threats per week.

They used to scare me, but now I just accept it as part of the price of being an influencer."

Steve clucks his tongue. "Well, you'd better take these guys seriously. They're looking to build a reputation, trust me. And for some reason they're fixated on you."

"Shh," I say, putting my finger to my lips. "They're talking again."

"The Aegis Order will save humanity from itself, no matter the cost. No one listens, unless there is pain. No one cares, unless there is blood. Nobody changes, unless there is..."

The image changes to one of me, my eyes crossed out with red x's and a red slash on my throat drawn in with marker.

"...death."

I nearly drop the phone, my hands are shaking so bad. Leslie takes it out of my nerveless grasp and I settle onto a stone bench, unable to speak.

"Now we definitely have to call the police," Leslie says. "I'm calling them right now."

Steve shakes his head. "What are the police going to do? It's not like they're going to assign protection twenty four hours a day. Charlotte's not that famous. No offense."

"None taken."

Then I get an idea. I take my phone back from Leslie and start typing in the search bar.

"What are you doing?" Leslie asks.

"There's this security agency I follow, one that's been used by Easton Ross herself. It's all a bunch of ex-military and spy type of guys who run it...what was the name?"

The website comes up and I smile.

"Platinum Security. If they can keep Easton Ross safe, surely they can do the same for me."

I hope.

**Read the full story: Stars and Scars**

## ALSO BY KELLY MYERS

**Platinum Security Series:**

Dark Kisses | Dark Riches | Dark Sins | Dark Secrets

**Platinum Security: Shadows of LA**

Stars and Scars | Silk and Steel | Glamour and Grit

**Dangerous Love Series:**

Tainted Goods | Brutal Love | Deadly Devotion | Twisted Truths

**Forbidden Love Series:**

The Guy Next Door | Arrogant Jerk | Misunderstood | My Best Friend's Ex | Office Mischief | Fool Me Twice

**Searching for Love Series:**

Against All Odds | Frenemies with Benefits | Breaking All The Rules | Fake Heartbreak

**Big Daddies of LA Series:**

Daddy's Rules | Daddy's Temptation | Daddy's Fake Fiancée | Daddy's Million Dollar Proposal

**Daddy Knows Best Series:**

My Secret Daddy | Yes Daddy | Forbidden Daddy | Billionaire Daddy | Daddy's Best Friend | Pregnant with the Wrong Man | Dirty Little Secret | Holiday Daddy | Daddy's Game

**Standalone Books:**

Ruthless | My Possessive Ranchers

# INVITATION TO JOIN KELLY'S NEWSLETTER

I love to weave steamy contemporary romance stories that ignite the imagination and stir emotions.

Join me for sizzling forbidden love tales where heat meets heart - from scandalous office romance to tantalizing age-gap love stories, and even sinfully suspenseful romance. With Happily Ever Afters, of course!

Explore the depths of passion, uncover hidden desires, and fall in love with unforgettable characters who will keep you turning page after page.

Sign up to my Newsletter -> kellymyersbooks.com/newsletter

Made in the USA
Middletown, DE
05 July 2025

10131808R00099